AXTIN

CONQUERED WORLD: BOOK TWO

ELIN WYN

CLOCK
WALK
PUBLISHING

LEENA

"You can't be serious!"

I clenched and unclenched my hands to stop them from shaking. It was all I could do to keep my voice even. I could feel my nails digging into my palm.

"Try to think about it logically, Leena," Mariella suggested. Her usually musical voice was grating. My temper flared and snapped, but I reeled it in.

"I'm the only one on this entire fucking ship capable of thinking *logically*," I spat. "You're insane for thinking you're safer on this ticking time bomb of a ship."

Why couldn't she understand? Technically, now that the *Vengeance* had a sustainable power source and the cloaking device was working, the Xathi couldn't see it. Nevertheless, I wouldn't call that safe because we still knew next to nothing about the aliens we'd been living alongside.

"I'm alive because Tu'ver brought me here," Mariella said. I scoffed.

"Who knows why he really brought you here? He could have intended to use you as a hostage...or a concubine," I sneered. I had to believe that Mariella was being willfully ignorant of the danger she was putting herself in, and me by extension.

"That's an ugly thing to say," she remarked with a bite in her mild voice.

She turned away from me to look at a false window with a holographic projection of a garden. Her dark wavy hair fell across her cheek.

"The longer we spend on this ship, the less time we have to find a cure," I said.

Mariella didn't look at me. She didn't speak. I stood for a moment, and let the familiar feeling of helplessness wash over me.

I rejected it, shoving it deep down inside me. If she wanted to act like a child, fine. I had other things to do, anyway.

I left the room without saying another word.

Earlier that morning, I'd been told that the captain of the *Vengeance,* General Rouhr, wanted to meet with me. I couldn't imagine why.

I didn't think he knew who I was. I certainly didn't

know who he was. I'd kept my contact with the aliens at a minimum since I arrived on this ship, unlike Mariella and the other woman, Jeneva.

Mariella preferred to spend her time looking at imaginary gardens and talking to Tu'ver. Jeneva was actually *with* one of the red ones now. If they wanted to risk their lives like that, who was I to stop them?

Sure as hell didn't mean I trusted any of them.

I strode through the sliding metal doors of one of the com rooms. General Rouhr, a rugged-looking Skotan with a scar running down the left side of his face, greeted me with a nod. My gaze flickered to the others in the room.

I was surprised to see Jeneva there. She smiled at me. I didn't smile back.

When I first met her, she was prickly and unfriendly. I didn't fully understand what had changed about her.

The Skotan she'd become enamored with sat next to her. I believed his name was Vrehx. He was the only one on the ship I didn't mind, and he had the good sense not to bother me.

My gaze settled on the hulking form of a green Valorni. Jagged purple bands stretched over his broad shoulders and along his thick arms.

Oh, hell.

This *creature* was a living, breathing personification

of a migraine. Axtin was brash, thickheaded, and impulsive—everything I hated. What the hell could he possibly be doing here?

"Ms. Dewitt, thank you for coming," General Rouhr said.

It was strange hearing him speak in my language. The ear transmitter, one of the things they'd given us when we'd first arrived, had somehow taught the aliens our language.

Once I learned I could understand them without the transmitter, I insisted they remove it. I didn't like the idea of alien tech crawling around in my brain—and it literally did crawl. I'd never forget the horrible way it felt when it was first inserted into my ear canal.

Mariella and Jeneva had elected to leave theirs in. Because of this, they knew considerably more of the alien's tongue than I did. I'd also made a point to avoid as much contact as possible, so there's that.

"Will this take long?" I asked tightly.

"Why? You've got somewhere else to be?" Axtin smirked. I didn't even dignify his response with a glare.

"I'll be as brief as possible," the general said with an understanding nod. "We've received a message from Duvest, the last city that was hit by the Xathi."

I remembered. It was a devastating attack. Duvest was the manufacturing capital of the planet, and many labs relied on the equipment produced there.

"It seems," he continued, "that there is a group of people working to develop a weapon against the Xathi —some kind of a scent bomb, as I understand it. However, they have run into some problems developing the formula. I've recommended you to them."

"Why?" I demanded. I hadn't told anyone about my work or my research. I clenched my jaw and squeezed my hands into fists, shoving my temper down.

"Mariella mentioned you studied chemistry," Vrehx offered. I cursed, low enough that only myself could hear it. Mariella had no right to talk about my life to them.

But despite my anger, the idea of working again sent a jolt of excitement down my spine. I missed being in a lab. I felt more at home there than anywhere else.

Regardless of my distrust of the aliens around me, I did want this war to end. I wanted the Xathi gone.

"Do you have more information?" I asked General Rouhr.

He slid a thin data pad across the table to me. Displayed on the screen was a detailed plan for the bomb and several potential chemical formulas. I could already see a few places where the formulas could be improved.

I wondered what their lab setup was like. The city

was hit pretty hard. I doubted they had as much as they needed.

What supplies were available to them? Who was working on this? How did they know for sure that the Xathi are sensitive to smells?

"I can see the crazy wheels turning in her head," Axtin muttered.

I resisted the urge to throw the data pad at him. He was right, anyway. My mind was whirling, and it felt amazing.

Another thought struck me...

If the people in Duvest were able to send these notes, then they had network access. There was a chance, albeit a small one, that I could recover my own research notes from their lab. And if their lab was as good as I hoped it was, I could remain in Duvest to work on finding a cure.

"I'd be happy to help." I smiled at General Rouhr. He blinked once, the only indication that he was surprised by my quick response.

"Excellent," he responded. "I'll send a message back telling them to expect you. Jeneva?"

Jeneva pulled out a map of the region and laid it flat on the table.

"I took the liberty of marking out the quickest and safest way to get there," she explained. She swiped a hand over the map, and a three-dimensional holograph grid rose up between us. A glowing blue line snaked across the map, marking my theoretical path.

"This way avoids any known animal breeding grounds, environmental instabilities, and other hazards," Jeneva continued.

Though I didn't know much about her, I knew she lived in the wilds of the forest alone for an impossibly long time. I had enough good sense to take her word for it when it came to matters of survival.

"That doesn't look too bad," I ventured.

Duvest wasn't as far away as I'd thought it was. If I stuck with Jeneva's path, I'd be fine.

Besides, I wasn't completely helpless out in the forest. I'd managed to track down Mariella in the dingy backwater she'd been living in.

Before I could stop myself, I imagined what it might have been like if I hadn't decided to find her.

Would the aliens have found her? Would she even be alive now? Would *I* even be alive now?

I forced my mind to go quiet. Making room for those thoughts wouldn't do me any favors.

Mariella was alive. I was alive. That's all that mattered.

"I think it'll take the two of you a little more than a day to get to Duvest," Jeneva went on, completely unaware of how quickly my heart was beating.

"Two?" I asked, almost missing what Jeneva said.

"You didn't think we were going to send you out there alone, did you?" Vrehx chimed in, his brow furrowed in what might have been true concern...or maybe he just thought I was stupid. It was hard to tell with him.

"She wouldn't last an hour out there alone," Axtin scoffed, folding his arms across his broad chest.

I wasn't keen on making that trek alone, but now I wanted to show that arrogant prick I could.

"You're right," General Rouhr agreed. I bristled before I noticed something like amusement gleaming in his eyes. "That's why you'll be going with her."

"What?" Axtin and I blurted at the same time.

"He'll get us killed before the *Vengeance* is even out of sight!" I exclaimed.

That moron sought out a fight whenever he got the chance. He'd lead me right into a den of some awful, poison-spitting monster just for the fun of it.

"I want both of you ready to depart within the hour," General Rouhr commanded, completely ignoring our protests. "Dismissed."

AXTIN

Great. I have to play babysitter. So be it.

G My thoughts about this whole thing ranged from joy at being able to do something again and pure hatred at the idea that I was playing bodyguard to this...female.

Srell.

I took the slow way down to the armory, not wanting to give her the satisfaction of thinking that I rushed on her account. I punched in my code and took in a deep breath of that beautiful aroma.

How I wish they'd just let me sleep in here. Why won't they allow me to keep more than a blaster in my personal quarters? I mean, I understand the need to keep an accurate inventory and all, but dammit, why can't I keep my toys with me? Huh? What's so bad about that?

I looked around at what was easily my second favorite room, right behind the training facility.

To my left were the blasters, rifles, Tu'ver's personal sniper rifles, our ever-dwindling stash of grenades and smoke bombs, and some hand-to-hand weapons. The wall in front of me was where the packs and survival gear were kept.

I went there first, ignoring my little corner to the right. I grabbed two packs and loaded them with rations, ammunition, sleep packs, and med kits. Thinking about how small Leena was, I took more of the ammo and rations, giving myself the heavier pack.

Making sure I didn't forget anything, I turned to my corner.

Oh, the memories and toys!

I'm not like Tu'ver. I don't have built-in augmentations like his people do. But I did like the idea of being augmented when necessary.

Wonder if I need any of them now...

I spent a few minutes trying to decide if I needed my augments or not, then decided to just grab weapons and go. I grabbed my three blasters, strapping one to my left hip, one to my right hip, and the other behind my back. Then I grabbed my rifle, double-checking it and leaning it against the packs, and then I reached for my pride and joy.

She was a work of art, handmade over hundreds of

hours, thousands of tiny changes to make her *just* right, and dozens upon dozens of designs and alloy combinations to get the weight exactly the way it was.

I loved my hammer. It was massive, even I needed both hands to wield her. She had cost me a fortune just finding the right metals that were both lightweight and super strong.

Her handle was wrapped in a combination of Tyit leather and a Skotan fabric, giving me a super tight grip no matter how sweaty or bloody my hands get. She was the perfect close-range weapon against the Xathi. I could crack one of those bastards open with a single swing.

I put on the special harness I had made for her, then strapped her to my back.

I need to name you one of these days, I thought as I grabbed a sonic-net and a thigh-pack of grenades.

I made sure to double-check everything again just to make sure before I headed down to the cargo bay we were using to leave the ship.

There she was, waiting impatiently for me. When she saw me, she gave me this *hurry up* look, then stomped over towards the bay door, ignoring her sister as she passed by her.

Hmm, not that I care, but I wonder why she's ignoring her now after she was so insistent on staying with her before.

I caught up to her, handing her pack to her as I walked by to open the door.

We walked out, the door closed behind us, and we headed out. It was excruciating walking in silence—I couldn't stand it.

"Why didn't you say goodbye to your sister?" I asked, trying to break the ice.

Oh, the look she flashed me. If we could *weaponize* that look, the war with the Xathi would be over faster than we could process the idea.

"What does it matter to you?" she answered, obviously annoyed.

I could surmise that I had angered the female. "Honestly? It doesn't. I was just trying to make small talk."

"Well, you failed...miserably." *You think?* "Not that it's any of your business, but there's no point in saying goodbye to someone you're going to see again anyway."

"Okay," I said, putting my hands up to show that I was harmless. She stormed on ahead, leaving me to catch up. As I caught up to her, she looked me up and down, making me wonder if she was sizing me up for approval or not.

"So, why aren't you wearing that...that...disguise thing that you people have?"

"I don't need it."

"What the hell do you mean that you *don't need it?*"

I flashed her my sweetest smile and tried to put on a nonchalant face. "The whole planet is covered in different life forms, and your kind need to get used to the idea. That's why I don't need it. Besides, the people of..."

I tried to remember the name of the city we were going to. I was a little embarrassed by the fact that I couldn't remember the place. I was never good with names.

"Duvest," she said in a very mocking tone.

"Yeah. The people of Duvest already know about us anyway, so there's even less need to use it there."

I watched as she thought about this, then she shrugged and turned her back to me and started walking.

Hmm, not bad.

I shook my head, bit back a smile, and followed after her. We had barely been walking twenty minutes when she became a major pain in my rumpus.

She was stomping around, or at least it looked like she was stomping. She didn't bother being cautious of where she was walking, seemingly snapping every single twig, branch, and stick that was on the entire forest trail.

I was cringing at every snap, every crack, and every curse coming from ahead of me. Enough was enough. I had to say something.

"Excuse me... Um...excuse me? Miss no-sense-of-danger-or-understanding-the-need-for-quiet? Can we *not* step on every single branch in the forest or make an unreasonable amount of noise? Everything on your planet wants to kill everything else, and now the Xathi are here as well. So if you don't mind, I'd really like to not have to fight *everything* there is at every step."

I should have realized the mistake I made as soon as I started speaking, but I didn't.

"Excuse the shit out of me?" Her voice started to get a little higher with each word. "You've been on this rock only a short time, whereas I've been here my whole damn life. Don't you dare presume to tell me when I should and shouldn't be careful. Right now, we're nowhere near the *dangerous* parts of the forest. And as for your damn Xathi, that's what you're here for, isn't it?"

Srell, this woman was an aggravation, but she had a spirit that fit my people. She would have been a fine Valorni.

"Well? Isn't that why you're here? To *be* my bodyguard and fight off the monsters?" she asked.

"Yes. Yes, I am. Now, as your bodyguard, I suggest walking a bit quieter, a bit nicer, and maybe keeping an eye out around you for anything. With us and the Xathi here, this might not be a safe part of the forest anymore," I retorted.

"Fine."

She walked away from me again, but at least she was quiet about it this time. We walked for nearly an hour in silence before I made another mistake.

"I have an honest question for you," I asked.

With a normal voice that took me by surprise—I hadn't heard it from her before—she responded with a simple, "What's that?"

"All you have to do is double-check an equation for a formula, yes?" I confirmed.

"Yeah," she answered.

"Couldn't we have done that from the *Vengeance*? Why did we have to risk danger to travel there?" I followed up.

She stopped dead in her tracks, forcing me to stop and look back at her. The look on her face made me realize, finally, that I had made that mistake.

"Really?" she asked, clearly exasperated this time. "You think my job is *so* easy that I can just do everything remotely? That I don't need to be hands-on? That I can do it while sitting on the toilet? Is that what you think?"

"Well, no...I just..." I never got to say another word.

She went into an absolute tirade, ripping into me about my lack of intelligence, how I was just a jock—whatever that was—and how this was her life, her passion, and that she can't just *do* it from some room on a *god-forsaken alien trash can.*

She kept going for what seemed like forever before I heard something. I tried to quiet her, but she just took it as another dig at who she was and what she did and proceeded to get louder. I still heard the sound through the slight pauses in her verbal attack.

Something was coming.

Then they crashed out of the trees nearby, five of those Luurizi things—enough to be a herd. They were little *delicate* creatures, with poisonous barbs on their hooves. They jumped high in the air, their hooves aimed right at Leena's head.

They never made it there.

I caught one of the creatures, bounced it off the ground, and snapped its neck, turning its head clean around a full rotation.

Then I took my blaster and shot three of them in quick succession, knocking them back, rendering them immobile.

The remaining one changed its trajectory and then ran away as it saw its herd decimated.

"Oh my God. Oh my God." Leena kept repeating over and over, staring at the creature as it twitched on the ground.

I grabbed her and pulled her close, wrapping her in my arms. "I have you. I'll keep you safe."

Why am I letting myself feel for her like this? Why do I care about her own blasted feelings right now? She's annoying, she's stubborn, she's stupid—not really, she's brilliant, and she knows things I'd never hope to understand, but she's stupid on basic things—and she drives me crazy.

Then I noticed her eyes on me, her quickened breathing, and the look behind the shield she had put up. There was something there that I'd never noticed before. I chuckled to myself.

She was barely tall enough to reach my chest. Her blonde hair was in stark contrast to my brown, and her slim figure was dwarfed by my hulk. Something inside me screamed out to take her, to take her right now and make her mine.

Srell.

I knew right from that moment that there was something special about this female. But we had a job to do, and if we didn't get it done soon, there wouldn't be a chance for me to find out what. I pulled away from her.

I cleared my throat to get my voice back. "We should get going, before anything else shows up." I started walking.

LEENA

My hands shook, my breath coming in uneven gasps as I followed Axtin further down the path.

I told myself that it was the Luurizi attack, that I was just shaken from the near-death experience, but the lie felt hollow even in my own mind.

Sure, almost being impaled by a wild animal was unsettling—there was no denying that. But it was what I felt in Axtin's arms that had truly shaken me. Even then, walking several feet behind him, I could still feel him, the press of him against me, the heat of his emerald skin.

I groaned, shoving the thoughts from my mind with force.

Obviously, I reasoned with myself, the past few days

had affected me even more than I had realized. The trauma of everything had finally been catching up to me—sure, that was it.

Because clearly, I wasn't actually attracted to Axtin. For fuck's sake, he wasn't even a human being.

Feeling reassured of my relative sanity, I hurried my steps, closing the distance between us.

It wasn't exactly the simplest task. Axtin was, after all, a great deal larger than me. His long legs ate up the distance ahead of us, and I rushed to catch up to him.

I ignored the way my hands picked right up shaking as I got near him, just as I ignored the sound of my own pounding heart.

I had more important things to focus on after all, like save the world.

"Are you okay?" he asked, his voice quiet, gruff.

"Fine."

He turned his head slightly, eyeing me slowly. For a moment, I thought he'd speak, but he clearly thought better of it, turning his attention back towards the path.

I watched him from the corner of my eye, feeling unable to control my gaze. The sunlight played wonders on his skin, reflecting brilliantly off the deep green, off the bands of purple that stood in stark contrast to the rest of him.

He seemed to walk with extra care since the attack, his eyes constantly roving over our surroundings.

Every now and then, he'd quicken his pace, hurrying ahead to move a fallen log from the path or peek around a blind. His attention felt odd, personal somehow, and I found it almost impossible to look away.

It wasn't until his eyes met mine again that I even realized how long I'd been staring. Quickly, feeling like a child, I bowed my head, staring in rapt fascination at the thick carpeting of leaves beneath my feet.

I tried my best to focus on the real issue at hand, redirecting my thoughts back to the scent bombs. I had a fairly good memory of the formulas I'd already seen. If I could just focus on it, I might come up with a good solution before we even arrived in Duvest.

Try as I might, though, my thoughts seemed beyond my control. One moment, I'd be reciting a formula in my mind; the next, I'd find myself once again staring at Axtin's hulking form.

I groaned inwardly, frustrated at my own behavior for once.

What on earth was wrong with me?

We walked in silence for a long while, my thoughts twirling strangely through my mind. I don't know how long we went on like that. It seemed like hours, though I knew it was far less.

Axtin was the first to break the silence, slowing his gait to turn towards me.

"Are you sure you're okay?"

"I'm fine, Axtin. Why?"

"I just—" He seemed to stumble over his words, unsure how to continue.

"What?"

"I didn't do anything, did I? Like hurt or scare you, I mean."

I scoffed in amusement, completely caught off guard by the question.

"No, trust me. You couldn't, even if you wanted to."

He tilted his head, his features contorting into an expression I'd never seen on him before. He looked surprised, hurt even.

But more surprising than his reaction was my own. To my utter amazement, I immediately regretted my words. Sure, Axtin got under my skin from time to time —or most of the time. But it had never been my intention to hurt him.

I opened my mouth to tell him as much, but found myself at a loss for words. I had never encountered anyone who could make me trip over my own thoughts like this before. It was utterly infuriating.

I reached up, running my fingers through my hair in irritation as I struggled to come up with a coherent thought.

I was just opening my mouth to try again when the sound reached my ears.

My teeth slammed shut with an audible click, my head whipping around wildly in search of the source.

"Leena." I heard Axtin say, but my attention was elsewhere.

Somewhere, near from the sound of it, someone was crying—a child.

I spun in a circle, searching the trees as my heart started to thump wildly in my chest.

What would a child be doing all the way out here?

Had the Xathi found them?

After a moment that felt like an eternity, I stilled, focusing on the direction I was now sure the sound was coming from.

"It's coming from over there," I said, pointing towards a dense thicket.

"Leena, it's not—"

I didn't wait to hear what he had to say—I couldn't. With every passing second, my fear only seemed to grow. I knew something was wrong, and I couldn't simply stand around and talk it out with Axtin.

I surged forward before I'd even fully decided to, my feet kicking up clouds of dirt as I propelled myself into the thickening forest. With every step, the sound seemed to grow louder, beckoning me on like a siren.

My mind spun through a million possibilities for what might lay ahead, each grimmer than the last. I clenched my fists, struggling to find a sense of control in the sudden chaos.

I could hear Axtin calling my name from somewhere back in the trees, his voice laced with near panic. I understood his worry, feeling a deep sense of dread pool in my own chest, as well.

Still, I raced onward, unwilling to let my growing fear stop me. Somewhere in these trees was a child in need of help. I could never look at myself the same way again if I didn't do anything to help the poor thing.

The trees thinned around me, space opening up in the dense foliage. The cries grew even nearer, seeming impossibly close.

Finally, panting, I broke into a small clearing. My body quivered from the exertion, sweat beading my forehead as I looked wildly about for the source of the cries.

I was so panicked, I nearly missed her. She sat in the shade of a nearby tree, her dark hair was matted, falling around her in waves as she buried her face in her hands. The cries only seemed to grow louder as I approached, one hand extended before me in what I hoped would be seen as a sign of peace.

"Hello? Don't be afraid. I want to help," I said.

She didn't move, didn't say a word. Her cries continued unabated, her small shoulders shaking in the intensity of her pain.

"Are you hurt?" I asked softly, still inching my way towards her.

Still nothing. It was like she didn't even know I was there.

"Everything's going to be okay. I'm going to help you." I was nearly whispering, trying my best not to frighten her as I finally closed the distance between us.

I should have known that something was wrong—the way she ignored me, the way she seemed utterly oblivious to my presence. It should have been obvious that things weren't what they seemed.

My own fear made me completely unaware, though.

"Sweetie?" I asked, reaching down to touch her.

I expected her to jump, maybe even to scream at my touch, but she didn't—though I suppose that makes sense, given that I never touched her at all.

My hand passed neatly through her, disappearing into the pale white of her shoulder. I felt nothing—no resistance, nothing.

My thoughts seemed to stutter, logic failing me in my shock.

I reached for her again, only to watch my hand pass once more through the shaking child at my feet.

I looked around dazedly, feeling my eyes widen in fear.

And that's when the walls went up around me.

The forest floor sprang to life, beams of energy

seeming to jump from the earth itself. I was instantly encased, trapped on all sides by the neatly spaced beams that created a wall around the air.

Time seemed to slow as my mind spun painfully, desperately trying to make sense of this newest twist. In utter horror, I took in the cage that now surrounded me, my gaze whipping from it to the still sobbing child now safely outside of its walls.

My thoughts seemed to slow even as my heart began to race.

That's when I started to scream.

AXTIN

There was a moment, the smallest fraction of a second, where I couldn't imagine Leena making that sound.

I couldn't picture her making such a noise. The pure terror, the anguish, drove me into a blind rage. Not even the trees were safe as I tore a path through the dense undergrowth to reach her.

I didn't understand it. Yes, I had orders to protect her, and regardless of how much of a pain in the ass she was, I was going to fulfill those orders. I'm not going to pretend I'm easy-going; I'd just as likely shoot something before talk to it.

But this aggression, this blood-boiling rage, was irrational, even by my standards.

If it was anyone else, I would have scoffed. It was

their fault for being careless. I warned them, and they should have listened to me.

Of course, I'd help them, but I probably would have been a bit of an ass about it. But not with Leena. All I wanted was to find her and get her somewhere safe.

Leena was caught in a spring-trap cage with a force field keeping her in. I shook my head in disgust. I'd seen this too many times.

Leena clawed at the invisible barrier frantically, still trying to reach for the child—rather, the holographic projection of a child. Each time, the energy feedback crackled and pushed her back.

Quickly, I looked and found a rock, throwing it into the force field. Energy shards went in all directions, lighting up the surroundings. Still, the force field stood.

I took my blaster and began to unload on it. It flickered furiously. I continued my firing until the force field finally winked out.

Leena was still shrieking, her eyes wide, but not fully seeing what was happening around her. I pulled her into my chest, trying to stabilize her.

For the second time that afternoon, we were incredibly close. And for the second time that day, I realized she was not as indestructible as she made herself seem to be. The living ice statue of a person I'd been bickering with was just a cold exterior—I didn't have a clue what she was really like.

"Make it stop! Make it stop!" she moaned, trashing against me and pounding on my chest with her almost comically small hands.

The hologram was still activated, the false child still crying for help. Still keeping Leena close, I kicked away at the layer of dead twigs and rotting leaves until I found the small hologram generator. It made a satisfying crunch when I smashed it under the heel of my boot.

It had been a while since I'd seen a hologram lure like that. If I hadn't been trained to recognize them, it would have fooled me the same way it did Leena.

"It's gone now," I said, wrapping an arm around Leena's small shoulders. She wasn't fighting against me anymore, but her breathing was rapid and shallow, and her eyes still darted around like she was still searching for the human child.

I reached up and gently caught her face in one of my hands, forcing her to look at me. It was easy to forget how small she was when she had such a large presence. She put so much effort into making herself seem bigger and scarier than she actually was.

"Leena, listen to me," I said gently but firmly. "That child wasn't real. It was a hologram."

"What?" she rasped.

"It was a Xathi hologram lure," I explained. "So right now, we have to get moving. If there are any Xathi in the area, they'll be heading this way to see what set it off."

That seemed to snap Leena back into it. She nodded once before stepping out of my arms.

"Which way?" she asked.

I jerked my chin vaguely towards the path of destruction I'd left behind me when I rushed to help her. She nodded again but didn't start walking until I was in step with her.

We walked quickly and quietly for about a mile. When I was sure the Xathi were no longer an immediate threat, I reached out and touched her arm.

She flinched at first, fixing me with a cold stare that didn't have its usual bite behind it.

"I just want to make sure you're okay," I told her, lifting my hands in a surrendering motion. She softened a bit.

"You said that thing was a Xathi hologram," she started to speak, not answering my question. "How did they make it?"

I didn't say anything at first. The answer to her question wasn't a pleasant one.

"Axtin," she said, the annoyance I'd become used to rising in her voice, but now it was tinged with dread.

"They record them from real people," I responded, looking at the ground.

She'd stopped walking. I didn't want to see her

expression. It was rare for me not to want to look someone in the eyes.

"What happened to the child they took the image from?" she asked further, her voice low and quiet.

I had a feeling she already knew the answer, so I remained silent. She didn't like that. I heard the sound of her stomping towards me, closing the distance between us.

I lifted my gaze to meet hers.

Her eyes were brimming with tears that she was using every ounce of her willpower to stop from falling. She was working her hands again, opening and closing her fists. Her jaw was set in that stubborn way of hers, but I could see her lower lip trembled.

The urge to kiss her rose up in me once more, but now was not the time. I could see that she wasn't going to let it go. For whatever reason, she wanted to hear me say it out loud.

"When the Xathi target a species, they use these lures to break a population—a psychological form of torture, if you will," I explained. It was easy to say if I thought about it like I was reading a mission dossier. Forewarned is forearmed, or some crap like that.

"They target the offspring of the species," I went on, "knowing the adults will go to extreme lengths to keep their children safe. It disrupts organization, demoralizes spirits, and troubles minds. They can traumatize a whole population by threatening the children."

"That's horrible," Leena gasped. She wrapped her slender arms around herself and shifted uncomfortably. "How do you know all this?"

"I've seen it before," I replied, looking down at the forest floor once more. "I've seen it more times than I can count, actually. It's never easy to see. The holograms are incredibly lifelike, but there's always something just slightly *off* about them. That's the only way to tell if it's real or not."

"Did," she started, but then she stopped herself, second-guessing her words.

I don't think I'd ever seen her second-guess anything before. I could have guessed where she was going with this.

"Did it happen to your people?"

"Yes," I answered directly. There was no point in dancing around it. It wasn't like I could change what happened. "We stole all of the holograms we could find once we figured it out, but by that time, they'd already done a lot of damage. We studied them and eventually used them for training."

"Training?" Leena clarified. She struggled over the word as if she had a million other things she wanted to say—and knowing her, she probably did—and that was the first word to make it out of her mouth.

"Desensitizing, mostly," I continued. Most of the other Valorni aboard the *Vengeance* had been through similar training. It wasn't something we talked about under any circumstances.

"One soldier lost his mind because the hologram image was taken from his sister's child. But the rest of us became adept at telling the real children from the holograms. So I guess, overall, it was a good thing. Saved a lot more lives on both ends."

Sometimes I could even convince myself it was all just some profoundly fucked up dream I'd had. But now that I'd started talking about it, I realized I didn't want to stop. It was like slicing open a wound to let the poison seep out—painful, yet oddly relieving.

One look at Leena's face made me wish I hadn't said anything. She looked five shades paler than usual.

I quickly glanced down at her hands. She was digging her nails into the palm of her hand again. I reached out to grab one of her hands, to make her stop, but she pulled away.

"What happens to the children the Xathi take the holograms from?" she pressed on, her eyes burning so intensely it would have made a lesser man recoil.

"Leena—"

"Tell me!" she shrieked loud enough to startle a flock of colorful birds out of the trees above us.

I was tempted to shush her but instantly thought

better of it. If by some miracle she didn't attract some insane monster to rip us to shreds, I suspected she would tear me apart herself.

"The child in that hologram is probably already dead," I stated bluntly. I hated telling her something so awful, but I knew she'd hate it even more if I tried to sugarcoat it.

I realized that Leena liked dealing with simplified information, much in the same way I did. It was easier to digest things when they were stripped down to their bare bones and less messy.

I thought she couldn't get any paler, but I was quickly proven wrong as she turned as white as a sheet. Her legs began to shake as the horrible truth of this stupid war closed in around her. I suspected she'd been trying to emotionally distance herself from everything, a good tactic for a soldier, but she wasn't one.

"Leena, you're looking unwell," I told her gently, taking a slow step towards her.

"I'm fine," she snapped, but she was swaying on her feet. This was really hitting her hard.

"No, you're not," I sighed. "How about you swallow that pride of yours and let me help you before you end up with a mouth full of dead leaves."

"Touch me and I'll break your wrist," she threatened.

I laughed. "How about this?" I said, taking three big steps backward. "If you can walk to me, I'll let you *try* to break my wrist." She glared at me, which I took as a good sign, before taking one step. She wobbled.

"That's what I thought," I said, closing the distance between us and scooping her up in one swift movement. "I'm starting to believe you would literally rather die than ask for help. That's going to get you killed long before the Xathi ever find you."

"Next time *you* ask someone for help, let me know and I'll take notes," she grumbled.

LEENA

"You can put me down now," I said for the fifth time since Axtin started carrying me.

It took longer than I was willing to admit to stop feeling like the world had been ripped out from under my feet. And I sure as hell wasn't going to tell him that I still felt sick and dizzy every time I thought of that poor child.

"I actually like this," Axtin said with that insufferable smirk plastered on his face. "It beats having you stomping around, alerting every living thing within a three-mile radius of our presence. You'd think someone as tiny as you wouldn't have the force to make so much noise. And yet…"

I think he was trying to make me laugh—or at least distract me from everything that had happened today. I still didn't know what to say to him after what he told me. Just seeing one of those holograms was horrible for me.

I can't imagine what it was like, seeing them over and over again, knowing that those children weren't going to get to go home to their families ever again.

Axtin was the most arrogant, impulsive, boorish person I'd ever encountered, but now...I was beginning to think that there was much more to him than what meets the eye.

"I think you're just looking for an excuse to flex," I retorted.

"Oh, please, I've carried gear packs heavier than you," he shot back with laughter in his voice.

Above us, the last light of dusk filtered through the thick canopy. Slowly—so slowly, I didn't even notice at first—the forest began to glow.

Patches of phosphorescent blue, green, purple, and pink sprung up on every trunk. Leaves were mottled with glowing beads.

"Wow," Axtin said quietly, craning his neck to look around.

"There are over thirty-five species of bioluminescent mosses and fungi," I offered. "No one has figured out why they developed bioluminescence, but that doesn't make them any less pretty."

"No kidding," Axtin said as a swarm of tiny silver insects swirled around us.

Suddenly, I didn't mind being carried by him. It gave me a chance to take in the natural beauty of the deadly forest.

It was widely known that wandering the forest after dark was foolhardy, but I don't think that rule applied to someone like Axtin. I didn't know as much about the creatures that inhabited the forest as Jeneva, but I couldn't think of anything that Axtin wouldn't be a fair match for.

"How much farther?" I asked absentmindedly. Part of me was still so eager to get to Duvest, to see the lab and finally have some work to do. But the other half of me didn't want to leave the glowing forest.

This place reminded me of the stories my mom used to read to me and Mariella. Stories about a time before magic turned into science, when mysteries were exciting, not deadly.

"Farther than I would like," Axtin said, twisting a bit to look at the navigation device on his wrist. "I was hoping we'd reach Duvest by nightfall. Obviously, that's not going to happen. We're going to have to find shelter for the night."

"I think the forest is bright enough for us to keep going," I said thoughtfully.

"Sure, it's bright enough for us to see big things like

those hulking trees that walk around," he said with a shudder. "I'm sorry, but trees shouldn't walk. They're breaking, like, twelve natural laws."

I laughed, rolling my eyes.

"But in this light," he continued, "I don't think I could tell the difference between the real vines and the ones that want to strangle us. Can you?"

I thought about it for a moment. If I were being honest with myself, I may have overestimated my ability to handle myself in the forest, especially after that unfortunate run-in with the Luurizi.

When I didn't answer right away, Axtin spoke up. "Deadly and confusing wildlife aside, you had a pretty bad scare today. There's nothing better for something like that than a good long sleep." He gave me a gentle squeeze.

"I don't think this forest can offer a good, long sleep," I replied.

"Either way, we're going to have to make something work," he shrugged.

We moved in silence for a while as he scanned the area for any place that could be used as shelter for the night. I was about to suggest climbing a tree and sleeping in shifts when I felt Axtin slow down.

"That fallen tree looks big enough for both of us." He jerked his head towards a massive tree that must have fallen years ago.

The inside of the tree was completely hollowed out. I doubted it was natural—but I didn't want to think about what sort of creature could hollow out an entire tree. The huge thing was covered in a blanket of bioluminescent moss that shifted from blue to green and back again, surrounded by other trees that were still standing, shot through with veins of glowing purple.

It looked beautiful.

Axtin set me down at the mouth of the hollowed-out tree. It looked wide enough for both of us, but just barely. I sank down to my hands and knees and crawled in.

Without the sun, the natural dampness of the forest made me feel a little cold. I was grateful when Axtin crawled in after me. In the small space, he was essentially a space heater.

I kept my body rigid, my shoulder pressed up against his arm. In the last twenty-four hours, I'd been in closer contact with him more than I had with anyone in the last five years.

I was consumed with my work, my research. I willingly refused all romantic attention. Without the cure, what was the point? I couldn't fall in love with anyone, I couldn't marry anyone or start a family knowing that I would die far too soon and pass on my curse to my children.

"I swear I can almost feel you thinking," Axtin groaned. He rolled over onto one side so that his chest was pressed against my arm. "Relax, would you? Nothing is going to grab you and drag you off into the night. I promise."

"I wasn't even thinking about that...but now I am," I hissed.

Axtin laughed, still trying to shift into a more comfortable position. His body pressed harder against mine. I tensed.

"You're stiffer than the damn tree," he sighed. "If you're not going to relax, will you at least roll onto your side?"

"You should have picked a wider tree," I huffed as I rolled over.

Well, I *tried* to roll over so that my back was to Axtin, but my face was uncomfortably close to the dank inside of the tree. So, I rolled again, only to gasp upon realizing we were face-to-face. Our noses were less than an inch apart.

"What are you so afraid of?" he asked suddenly.

I could see his eyes shining in the darkness. The light from the glowing plants outside faintly illuminated his features.

"Excuse me?" I bristled.

"I mean, besides the genocidal aliens invading your planet and the forest where everything wants to kill you," he continued.

"I'm not afraid of the forest," I bristled.

"Right," he snorted.

"What makes you think I'm afraid of anything?" I snapped.

"You fight so hard to have control over everything," he said. "In my experience, people only do that when they're afraid."

"You're so full of shit," I said. "I don't need to be in control of everything."

"Prove it," Axtin challenged. Even in the dim light, I could see his smirk. "Relax your body."

"I don't have to prove anything to you," I said dismissively.

"No, you don't. But if you don't relax, you're going to be in bad shape tomorrow," he shrugged. He closed his eyes, and within a few minutes, his body went slack.

Never in my life have I been able to fall asleep that quickly. I was kind of jealous.

I didn't like the idea of being the only one awake. I felt stupid and childish as I nudged Axtin.

"Don't worry—I'm not asleep yet," he said smugly.

"Oh," I said quietly.

I didn't know what to say. I didn't know what to do. I felt strange. My brain felt sluggish and stupid.

"Was there something you wanted to talk about?" he

asked. "Or are you just keeping me awake for the fun of it?"

"I just...I don't think I ever thanked you for saving me. Twice." I struggled with my words. Admitting that he saved me was like admitting my dependence on him.

I prided myself on being dependent on no one—but that mindset was what put us in danger in the first place. "So...thank you. And I'm sorry for what the Xathi did to your people. That must have been horrible."

"Yeah. It was," he said curtly. "But there's nothing I can do about that now except for trying to help you and your people."

"We're lucky to have you fighting for us," I said quietly.

I couldn't meet his gaze. I almost jumped out of my skin when I felt his hand brush through my hair.

"Easy," he soothed. "You're so tightly wound. How can you even function?"

"I manage."

"Barely." His hand grazed my cheek and gently traced down my neck.

My eyelids fluttered, and a small sigh escaped my lips. His hand traveled over my shoulder, down the bare skin of my arm, to rest at the small of my back. Very gently, he pulled me in closer.

My body felt loose, my chest pressed up against his.

He dipped his head, letting his lips lightly press into my neck.

And then I felt his cock. Thick, massive, and throbbing.

Much larger than anything a human male could ever field.

Just like that, my body went rigid again.

"What are you afraid of? It's just a kiss," he teased, though he didn't try to do it again. He lifted the pressure off the small of my back. He was letting me get away if I wanted to.

But I didn't want to. The realization hit me like a bolt of lightning.

Before I let myself think about it, I reached up and pulled his face closer to mine. I brought my lips to his in one smooth motion. My control stopped there.

With a growl, Axtin pressed his body against mine, trapping me between himself and the inside of the tree trunk. He kissed me hard, one hand snaking around my waist, the other winding into my hair.

To my surprise, I didn't feel panicked. I knew Axtin wouldn't hurt me. Pressed between him and the tree, I realized I had given him full control. The relief was immense. The rush of heat, desire, and raw emotion undid me.

In the span of a moment, I'd become insatiable.

Axtin kissed his way down my neck and bit the

tender slope of my shoulder. I cried out from the wonderful mix of pain and pleasure.

"Did I hurt you?" he moaned into my skin.

"Do it again," was my only response.

With a growl, he sunk his teeth into me again, harder this time. He shifted us so that he was as on top of me as he could possibly be in our cramped quarters. The rough wood beneath me jabbed at my spine, but it only added to the intense flurry of sensations that engulfed me.

"Your scent is maddening." His voice was a deep rumble that I felt to my core.

He pressed himself into me. I could feel his considerable length pushing against my thigh. I tried to lock my leg around his waist to pull him closer, smashing my knee against the side of the tree in the process.

"Shit," I winced.

"We're going to get hurt if we keep going," he panted, his grin reaching from ear to ear.

I felt lightheaded. I wanted more. After years of shutting out all feeling, I craved this intensity. I couldn't imagine going another moment without it. I didn't care that my shoulder blades were barking in protest or that I could already feel the bruise forming on my knee.

"But—" I started to protest, but he put a finger to my lips.

"Leena," he said softly. "I've imagined taking you a hundred times. Not once was it in a half-rotten tree in the middle of the woods. Once we're somewhere safe and comfortable, I will make you mine."

His words sent a delicious shudder down my spine. All I could do was nod in agreement. He rolled us again so that I was lying on his chest. His arms were wrapped securely around me.

My body was practically humming. Warm and safe, I fell asleep in Axtin's arms.

AXTIN

The sun had barely started to break through the thick canopy of trees overhead when we woke, the faint light already smothering the bioluminescent glow that surrounded us only hours before.

We crawled from our shelter, blinking to clear the fog from our minds. We still had a ways to go before reaching Duvest, and Leena seemed to practically vibrate with impatience.

I knew that she was eager to help fight the Xathi. In fact, I don't think that anyone could relate more than me.

Still, though, her intensity was surprising. Just the day before, I would have said she'd rather face a Xathi horde alone than trek through the forest with yours truly, and it was a sentiment I would have gladly echoed.

In the light of the new day, though, she seemed even more intensely focused than I was, her steps rushed as we resumed our hike towards Duvest.

How things change.

We walked in silence, our breathing the only consistent sound in the air. More than once, I thought to break the quiet, but every time I opened my mouth to speak, something stilled me.

Leena was different today. Distant. And, for some reason I didn't quite understand, I felt the need to give her the silence she clearly craved.

As usual, I could see the wheels spinning in her mind. She was clearly lost in thought. Whether about the scent bombs or something else entirely—us, for example—I couldn't say.

I knew that getting so close to me the night before might shake her. It wasn't surprising, really—the female had despised me just hours before. I was more than happy to let her stew in her own thoughts...given, that is, that I expected she'd come to the right conclusion in the end.

So far as my own thoughts were concerned, I had already made sense of them the night before.

Leena was a pain. Srell, that was putting it lightly.

But she was also strong and passionate—the kind of female the Valorni knew better than to take for granted.

More than that, though, she was *my* female, and I would tolerate much more than her silence in order to please her.

After having seen her let loose, even to the extent that she did, I felt deeply protective of her. She had become my responsibility, and I wanted nothing more than to care for her.

The remainder of the trip passed quickly, both of us too invested in our thoughts to note the passing time. Sooner than I had thought possible, the hazy outline of Duvest appeared before us.

"Is that it?" I asked, my voice sounding strange after the prolonged silence.

"Yep, that's Duvest."

I gestured before us, encouraging her to take the lead. Sure, the humans were aware of us now, but I was fairly certain who they'd rather see coming towards them first.

My own view may also have crossed my mind, but I decided not to voice the thought. Some things should be cherished in silence, anyway. Even I knew that.

I followed Leena up the widening path, still taking pains to check our surroundings as we neared the city. We made it to the gates without any attacks, the guard posts disturbingly empty. As we passed into the city proper, only angry looks hindered us.

I ignored the glares, focusing instead on the female before me. I hadn't embarked on this particular journey with any expectation of open arms. They could all snarl and stare as much as they wanted—at the end of the day, it would still be aliens risking their lives to save the lot of them.

Leena found our destination without fuss, guiding us easily through the winding streets. We came to a stop before a midsized building.

"This is it," she said simply, pushing her way through the door.

The moment we stepped inside, I was certain we were in the right place. A million scents seemed to wash over us, their combination enough to make a lesser being feel ill.

"Smells like the right place," I said, giving Leena my most charming smile.

Nothing. Not even a smirk in return. She examined the room in silence before seeming to settle on a large male near the back.

"Excuse me," she said, crossing to him. "Are you in charge here?"

"I am, and who might you be?" His question was directed at her but his eyes fixed immediately to my position.

Leena glanced back, not missing the edge in the male's voice.

"I—we—are here to help. My name is Leena. I believe you were expecting me?"

His eyes seemed to clear. "Of course. You're here to help with the scent bombs."

She nodded, all business now. "Where can I get started?"

It took no time at all for her to find her place, and I watched in rapt fascination as she set to work. She and the male spoke for several minutes, exchanging words that even the ear worms hadn't prepared me to understand.

At some point in the conversation, Leena began to change. There was no anxiety in her now, no stress apparent in her expression. She seemed calmer than I'd ever seen her, laser-focused on the task at hand. It was intoxicating.

I approached as the male finally left her side, smiling down at her as she arranged strange glass vials onto the counter before her.

"Anything I can do to help?" I asked.

She looked up, her vision clearing as if she'd only just remembered my presence.

"Oh...um, no actually. I'm all set here," she answered.

"Are you sure?" I asked, looking for anything to keep

me busy around her. "It's not like I have anything better to do."

She shook her head. "Really, Axtin, I've got it handled. You don't have to babysit me if you don't want to."

"I'd rather not leave you."

The mere thought of letting her out of my sight bothered me. After last night, I wasn't sure I'd ever be able to leave her alone again.

She rolled her eyes—an expression that was becoming achingly familiar the more time we spent together.

"Really, Axtin, I'm fine here. I won't be able to work with you hanging over my shoulder, anyway. I'm sure you can find something to pass the time elsewhere."

I mimicked her eye roll, actually eliciting a little smirk from her. I knew there was no point in arguing, though—Leena was as stubborn a female as any I'd ever met, my own species included.

"Fine, but I'll be back to check on you," I warned.

"I'm sure you will."

She was already back to arranging vials, her eyes taking on a far-off, thoughtful look.

With a sigh, I turned, leaving her to her work.

There was clearly nothing for me to do in the building, so I headed for the door. I might not have known much about human science, but I was sure there would be something outside that I could busy myself with.

I stepped into the gradually brightening day, looking around for distractions. It wasn't long at all before I saw just the thing.

The city, like many back home, was enclosed on all sides by thick metal walls. There used to be an electric charge, but it appeared that the conductors were fried in the attack.

I stood for a moment, letting my gaze travel across them. I was sure that they were a great defense against the human's usual threats: walking trees and the like. But these beings had never had to face a threat like the Xathi before.

I walked to the nearest wall, running my hand along its rough surface as my mind whirled in thought. There was no way that such defenses would ever stand up to a Xathi horde without further reinforcing. Compared to Xathi weapons, their walls might as well have been toothpicks.

I ignored the glares that trailed me as I followed the structure, counting gun towers as I walked. They were at regular intervals, which was good, but they seemed woefully undermanned. Someone would need to talk with them, to explain the severity of the threat they were facing.

Ideally, that information would come from a trusted

source, but I knew that the task would almost certainly fall to me.

I groaned, running a hand through my hair as I mentally tallied the improvements that would need to be made, knowing full well that, even if they heeded my advice, they were still dangerously outgunned.

A female turned the corner in front of me, visibly starting when her eyes landed on my position. She froze in her tracks, her mouth popping open with shock.

I ignored her, turning my attention back to the wall.

I knew it was unlikely that anyone would take my advice seriously. Humans, I was learning, were an incredibly prejudiced species. They might eventually accept us here, but I worried that it might take more time than we really had to spare.

It's not that I judge them for their fear. In fact, I empathize with it. It was only a short time ago that most of them thought they were alone in the universe— and now their planet was crawling with "aliens". It was a lot to take in.

The issue, however, was that they really didn't have any choice but to accept this new reality. We were here, plain and simple.

And so were the Xathi. No amount of denial was ever going to change that. In fact, their refusal to adapt was likely to get them all killed.

"C-can I help you?" A voice piped up.

I turned to the source, finding a large male behind me.

His clothing suggested he was military of some sort, possibly a city guard. He stood tall for a human, though his head barely passed my shoulders. His face was pulled into a weary expression, his hand settled easily onto the handle of his blaster.

"Possibly. My name is Axtin. I'm here helping with the Xathi defense. What can you tell me about your fortifications?"

He was visibly taken aback, his eyes widening as he looked me up and down.

"Our fortifications?" he asked.

"Your defenses," I reiterated.

His brow furrowed as he took a step nearer. "You expect me to tell an alien about our defenses?"

Of course.

"If you want help," I answered, taking an answering step towards him. "And, to be honest, I think you could use all the help you can get."

That did it. His lips pulled back, revealing lines of yellowed teeth as his fingers tightened around his weapon.

"I don't know how things work where you come from, but around here, we don't just go giving intel to *aliens*." The last word he spat like a curse.

"I'm only trying to help."

He took another step towards me, rising onto his toes to better reach my level.

"Oh, you wanna *help.* That's perfect. You know what would really help would be if you and all your alien pals would just do us a favor and die."

My hands clenched at my side, nails digging into my palms as I willed myself to remain calm.

"What's your name?" I asked, resisting the urge to wrap my hands around the male's throat.

He didn't answer. Instead, he snarled, leaned back, and spit in my face.

I saw red, my vision blurring in anger as the enraged human turned his back on me. He didn't say another word, simply walked back the way he'd come, his steps so infuriatingly self-assured, it was all I could do not to run him down and destroy him.

I forced a breath into my lungs. Then another, not moving until I trusted myself not to pull the hammer from my back.

With slow, deliberate movements, I turned back towards the lab, wiping the spit from my face as I walked.

Somehow, I had actually underestimated the humans' hatred for us. It wasn't a mistake I would be making again.

Some hopeful part of me had thought that we could

all work together, that we could live alongside each other. Clearly, I had been mistaken.

We couldn't just coexist with the humans. Even those who wanted to would be shunned for accepting us. Like Jeneva...like Leena.

My breath caught at the thought.

Leena and I would never be accepted. If any of these people knew about the two of us, they'd have run us out of town already. There was no way we could be together.

Even if she were willing to tolerate the abuse we'd receive for our pairing, how could I let her?

My mind reeled as I reached the lab, taking a moment to calm myself before stepping back through the door. It was obvious to me now that Leena and I couldn't continue what we'd started.

I was a fool to ever think we could.

For her sake, we had to stop before things got any more serious.

LEENA

Walking into a lab was like walking into my own home. I inhaled deeply, relishing the smell of disinfectant and sanitation agents.

The equipment was not state-of-the-art like it was in my home lab. I hadn't expected it to be, especially since Duvest was attacked so recently.

Some of the machines looked like they had been pieced together from spare parts. I admired the ingenuity of these people, but poor equipment meant imprecise work. That may account for at least one of the problems they've had while trying to develop the scent bomb.

They had a spare lab coat for me. It didn't fit right, and it smelled used. I felt a pang in my chest as I thought of my closet full of pristine, perfectly-tailored, monogrammed lab coats.

I missed my house. I missed my spotless stainless-steel lab counters. I *really* missed the AI interface that could read results and run an analysis for me while I did something else.

But this would do. I still felt the same tingle I always felt when I had something to work on.

There was an organized, structured way to do this. There were rules to follow and methods to apply. This was my lab now—I was in control.

I wasn't like Axtin or Jeneva. Or even Mariella. They were all happy to fling themselves into the unknown to seek what they desired. They didn't mind braving inhospitable landscapes and hostile environments to find what they were looking for.

That sort of life never appealed to me. I preferred to be in here, with lab manuals and research notes, meticulously examining impossibly small samples, hunting down the slightest difference in their composition.

"This is the equation we've been working with."

My moment of self-indulgence was interrupted by a tall woman with skin the color of honey and an abundance of thick, dark hair.

I didn't understand why she was here—I already had

all of the research notes. I knew the equation. I already had several adjustments I wanted to test.

"Yes," I said. "It's likely to grow unstable the longer those elements interact with each other. I've come up with a few potential stabilizing agents, although I don't know what this lab has in stock."

"We don't have much," the woman said, stepping into my workspace. I tried not to grit my teeth.

She extended a hand. "I'm Rael, a professor at the campus here. Well, before the attack. Much of the grounds were destroyed, but I managed to salvage quite a bit from my old lab."

"That's a shame," I said. I didn't recognize her name. Usually, I knew the notable professors in the field. "Did you reconstruct the lab equipment yourself?"

"Mostly," she said with a proud grin. "I had some of the engineers help me with the wiring. It's not perfect, but it's a hell of a lot more than I thought we were going to have. I also have a list of potential stabilizing agents. The trouble, is we're going to have to make them ourselves."

She pulled up her list on a datapad and handed it to me. I was impressed—our lists were almost identical. Even if I had never heard of her, she seemed to know her stuff.

"It's a good start," I said genuinely.

I asked her to pull up a list of what the lab had in stock. It was disappointing.

"Essentially, we have to combine and separate these compounds over and over again until we have something that can fit into our equation without causing an explosion," I said.

"Or give off a toxic gas," Rael added.

"Or corrode skin," I chimed in with a smirk.

"Or harm civilians," Rael finished with a laugh.

I couldn't help but laugh, too. It was me and her against an impossible problem.

"What about notes on the Xathi?" I asked.

"Minimal," Rael replied. "After the attack, we were able to secure a few dead samples to analyze, but our equipment simply can't measure an alien lifeform the way we need it to. Everything about them—their blood, their brains—is completely unlike anything on this world. We decided on a scent bomb because their olfactory system was the only thing relatively normal about them."

"Aside from field testing," I shuddered, "how can we know if we're on the right track?"

"During the attack, a few citizens worked with the red alien to put a makeshift prototype together that had success in slowing the creatures down," Rael replied. "That's where we began to advance the research."

I nodded, remembering the stories.

"There was also a sonic weapon that had promise, but the problem was that, right now it affects humans almost worse than it would affect the Xathi. We need to spend more time developing and refining it, which will take much longer," Rael said.

"So, scent bombs are the only approach," I concluded.

"We were able to develop a simulation program," Rael explained, walking over to the computer. "It shows our best guess at how the Xathi process smells and how it affects their brain. We can input the equation and see what could happen."

"At least it'll help us narrow in on the right stabilizer," I said with a shrug.

It was guesswork at best. Ordinarily, I wasn't comfortable with guesswork. Especially when lives were at stake.

But there *were* aspects I could control. I could make this work—and I was determined to do so.

Rael and I worked for hours. Progress was slow, but I was happy. Rael was actually brilliant at what she did —she was a great partner to have in this. I possessed more technical knowledge than she did, but she was more creative when it came to testing compounds and using our limited resources.

With the new calculations in place, we ran the

simulator again. I watched as our creation interacted with the hypothetical Xathi body.

It went haywire on the Xathi's smell receptors. That in itself was an accomplishment. But it was what our calculations did to the Xathi's brain that made me want to jump around and cheer like a moron.

The simulated *brain* went haywire.

"I'm willing to bet that that will disrupt the hive mind," Rael said smugly.

I was beaming. This was *incredible*. I couldn't wait to tell Axtin about our progress.

Axtin. I'd been so focused on my work all day that I'd barely thought about him at all. Now that I had a chance to think about something other than the scent bombs, I realized that I was...excited to see Axtin.

I wanted to give him good news, give him a little hope that *this* world won't be lost the way his was.

"Now, we just have to make the stabilizing agent," I sighed, pulling my hair away from my face.

It was still a daunting task. We were missing several core components. It would take hours, if not days, to make it ourselves—if it could even be done.

"Ms. Dewitt." A man entered the lab, looking a little uncomfortable. "Your...escort is back."

"Send him in!" I grinned. Axtin appeared a few minutes later.

My smile faltered a little. There was tension in the

way he held his body. The corners of his mouth were pulled down. His eyes weren't glinting with a secret mischief.

"I have good news!" I said, not letting my own cheer diminish. He blinked in response. "Um...the equation. We fixed it."

I felt foolish now. Axtin's expression remained neutral.

I persisted. "We figured out that—"

"You know the details are lost on me," he cut me off.

My temper snapped like the end of a whip. Was I wrong for thinking he would care? There's no way he didn't understand how important this was.

I felt like I was missing a vital piece of information. I hated that feeling.

"Right," I said crisply. "I just thought you'd like to know. I'm sure General Rouhr is expecting an update."

"Let me worry about that," he replied, looking at the lab equipment rather than looking at me. I bristled.

"Actually," Rael interjected hesitantly. No doubt she could sense the sudden tension in the room. "When you do message your general, will you pass on my request to send you and Leena to Fraga with prototype scent bombs? Once we make them, of course," she added with a wink in my direction.

"Shouldn't you be asking me?" Axtin said, lifting his brows in arrogant surprise.

"Does your general ask before he gives you an order?" Rael quipped.

I liked her even more. Spending time with her made me miss the relationship Mariella and I had when we were children. We were always different, she and I, but we were always on the same side.

Now, I felt like no matter where I stood, Mariella placed herself as far away from me as she could. Chemical warfare I could handle, but the problems between me and my sister were outside of the realm of my control.

"I'll pass along your request," Axtin said curtly. "However, it will be in person when I deposit Leena back on the *Vengeance*."

"Excuse me?" I blurted.

"It's safer for you," Axtin explained. "And for me. I can handle whatever is in the forest. I can't keep track of you and ensure the scent bombs don't explode in our faces."

"Absolutely not," I said through clenched teeth. "This is *my* project. There is no way in hell I'm letting you take that from me. The only way the bombs would go off is if you were being careless—oh, wait, that's your natural state of being."

My words were spilling out before I could stop them. His indifference hurt me. But right now, I couldn't afford to be hurt. I constructed a wall of ice around my heart. That was the only way to ensure I wouldn't lose focus, that I would stay in control.

I was not going to give him the satisfaction of knowing he upset me.

But there was another reason why I needed to go to Fraga—there was a Quake station between here and there.

Many Quake stations were operated and maintained by the university. The computers here weren't linked up to a larger network, but the computers at the Quake station would be.

I had thought that there would be a way to create a connection in Duvest. But every method I tried to access my research failed when I attempted to connect to the university network.

If I could access my university network...there was a chance I could recover my research on my genetic illness.

I'd like to see Axtin try to keep me from it.

"Leena is qualified and authorized to handle the bombs," Rael interjected once more. "My apologies, but we can't allow anyone else to handle such delicate cargo."

Axtin wanted to fight her on it. I could see it writhing in his mind. But before he could start another argument, I spoke up.

"Why don't you go do your job and keep your

general informed? I have a lot of work to do. I'd appreciate it if you stopped distracting me," I said icily.

Axtin worked the muscles in his jaw before storming out of the lab.

What the hell was *his* problem? I bet that this was a little game he liked to play. He liked to seduce women just to leave them hanging. I bet he got off on watching them pine for him.

Well, not me! This was how I wanted it to be in the first place. I didn't even want him to come with me.

He was wild, dangerous, and unpredictable. He had no place in a lab, and he had no place in my life.

AXTIN

I woke up with a groan. The cot they gave me to sleep on was, by far, the most uncomfortable thing I've slept on in a *very* long time—and I live on a damn battle cruiser.

I couldn't believe she dismissed me like that. What the hell gave *her* the right to dismiss me so abruptly? All I wanted was for her to be safe—couldn't she see that?

I got up, and instantly regretted it. *That damn cot.*

My back was in pain, but I knew that a few good stretches would clear that up, so I put myself through a decent workout before I decided I needed food.

I grabbed a bite to eat from their cafeteria and ingested one of the most tasteless meals I've ever had.

Humans have no idea how to spice things. I need to teach them how to make a proper meal one of these days.

After eating, I asked around for Leena, but no one knew where she was. They knew where she *could* be, but not where she actually was. They said she was in the lab with Rael, they said she was in the manufacturing room, they said she was visiting with the mayor...she was everywhere and nowhere at the same time.

I was worried about her. Was she blowing me off? Was she angry with me?

So be it.

Let her be angry, I didn't care. Things were better for both of us if we didn't get involved. Her own kind would never accept her, me, or us, so it was just better to let it go.

I needed air.

I headed back into the city, intent on getting my head cleared and my mind right. The lab was located up a hill away from most of the city, and I took advantage of that height. I looked around the town, soaking in what I saw.

Duvest was a true manufacturing town. Many of the factories were located on the outer edges of the town, with warehouses nearby. Meanwhile, all the shops and businesses were located more to the center, with people's homes spread out everywhere.

Some people lived close to the warehouses and plants they worked at. Others lived above their shops. Then there were the neighborhoods out to the east.

If the Xathi were to attack again, they would attack the homes, drawing the people out into the open, making them easier to capture.

I hesitated. I didn't want to go into town because I didn't want to be around the humans—but I didn't want to be here, either.

Stop being weak, I thought to myself as I took in a deep breath of the morning air. It was cool, clean, and had a hint of moisture in it. It was nice.

I headed down into town, trying to stay in the sector with all the shops and parks. They were still repairing and rebuilding some of the damage caused by the last Xathi attack weeks ago, but they seemed to be in good spirits—until they saw me.

Conversations stopped as I passed by. People made a point to move away from me, and even in those that didn't move, you could see their discomfort.

I wanted to tell them I was safe. I wanted to tell them that I wasn't there to hurt them—I was there to help protect them.

I wanted to, but I kept my mouth shut. They wouldn't believe me. All they saw was a big man with green skin and lots of weapons.

And that scared them. Rightfully so. I could break most of these people in seconds, and they knew it.

I tried to clear my mind, stealing Vrehx's breathing technique. As I walked around, I paid little attention to the people around me.

They were the cause of my anxiety. They let their prejudice against the unknown run them, something I couldn't understand, not anymore. We had been a prideful race, believing ourselves better than all others.

Then the Xathi came. They devastated us, they embarrassed us, they killed us. If it wasn't for Rouhr and the others who taught us to put aside our hatred, we'd be an extinct race.

Without realizing it, I had wandered into a small park at the center of town. There were several families there, most of them with children.

The mothers grabbed their children. The few men there stood between me and them. They looked scared. Then, as several of the men took hesitant steps forward, I felt a little hand pulling at my leg.

It was a little boy, looking up at me with wide eyes filled with wonder.

"Excoos me, mista. Why is your skin gween?"

I chuckled. I was actually happy. I knelt down next to the boy. "What's your name, little warrior?"

"My name is Chucky. What's your's?"

"Hi, Chucky. My name is Axtin."

"Astin?"

"Yes." I smiled. This little boy was fearless. "To answer your question, my skin is green because that's a normal skin color for my people. See," I leaned in to whisper, "I'm what your parents call an alien. I'm not human."

"You're not hooman? Wow!"

The wonder on his face lit up my day. He turned towards the others, still standing there waiting to see if I was going to eat this little child or not.

"Mommy. He not hooman! He a aliem. He said his name Astin. Can I play with him?"

His mother stepped forward, slightly pushing one of the men to the side so she could get by. She had an infant strapped to her chest.

She looked at me, and I watched her visibly struggle to find her voice. "Are you here to fight those bug things?"

I nodded. "Yes, I am. They destroyed my people, and I'm trying to make sure they don't destroy yours, either."

"What will you do to my son?"

"Nothing." I looked down at him and smiled. "He's a brave little warrior, and I would be honored for him to teach me how to 'play.'"

Another of the women spoke up. "Why are you armed?"

I stood up, smiling at Chucky as I did. He grabbed

my hand and started pulling me towards the crowd. I didn't fight him.

"I was warned that some of your people might not be very welcoming to me, and I'm making sure that if the Xathi—the bugs—attack, I can fight back and protect you."

My non-threatening demeanor and the fact that Chucky was holding my hand seemed to loosen their tongues. The questions began pouring in.

Where did I come from? What was I? What are the Xathi?

Why are they here? Why are they attacking? What do they want from us?

How do we stop them? When are you leaving? How do we fight them?

I spent maybe three hours answering their questions as Chucky showed me how to play.

It made me feel like there might be a chance for me to be accepted, for me *and* Leena to be accepted.

As the families began to leave to go about their days, I said goodbye to Chucky, who tried to hold on to my hand for dear life. I smiled at him and told him I'd see him again. Only then did he let me go.

I actually missed the little warrior. I started walking around the city again, feeling good about myself and the potential for good relations with the humans.

I was in a jovial mood. Would that it would have

lasted. The city was busy, there were people walking the same direction as me, there were people getting out of my way and flashing me dark looks, but I wasn't letting it bother me.

I just thought about Chucky and his little smile, and things were fine.

Except for the human following me. I probably wouldn't have noticed them if they had just kept on walking whenever I looked back. But whenever I looked back to see what was behind me, I kept noticing one person that was trying to duck out of sight.

Fine, so I was being followed. Let them follow me.

I wasn't hiding anything. I wasn't threatening anyone. I wasn't even trying to look menacing.

I bought some food using some of the local currency that Leena had given me. I smiled, said thank you, and went about my way. It tasted better than breakfast. *Significantly* better than breakfast.

What did they call it? Currywurst? I loved the spices, the taste. And the meat that was used was fantastic. Very tasty. Maybe these humans *did* know how to cook.

I was still being followed as I enjoyed my meal. I wanted to turn around, find my stalker, and confront them, but I thought better of it. I didn't want to cause a scene around all these other humans.

I made a turn down another street where the foot

traffic was light, almost non-existent. The few people that were on the street looked at me in wonder but kept walking, leaving me be.

I shrugged. Not everyone was going to be nice like Chucky.

As I passed by an alley, I heard something. I stepped back, looked, and my blood instantly boiled.

Two men were assaulting a woman, trying to take advantage of her. Yelling to get their attention, I rushed down the alleyway, scaring them off. I spent a few seconds making sure they were gone, then turned back toward the woman.

She looked a lot like Leena—short and blonde—and she looked terrified.

"Don't worry. I won't hurt you," I said. "And I won't let them hurt you, either. My name's Axtin. Is there somewhere I can help you get to?" I tried to dial up a soothing, calming voice.

But she pulled back from me, called me a monster. I stood up straight and shook my head.

"Really? *I'm* the monster? I wasn't the one trying to hurt you, but *I'm* the monster". I shook my head. "Do you need help or not, female?"

It was her sudden smile that told me I was in trouble. "No. You've helped me enough."

She pointed something at me and pushed a button. Some sort of liquid sprayed out, and srell did it burn!

Then I heard the attack. Someone jumped on my back. I felt a pipe strike my left thigh, another pipe hit me in the arm, all while the person on my back pounded on my head.

I had no choice. I had to fight back. I wasn't going to let myself be killed or hurt by these idiots.

So, I fought back. I reached back and grabbed the one on my back and flipped them off of me. There was a nasty crunching noise and a high-pitched scream of pain.

I could barely see, but I could see enough. The shadow to my left swung their pipe again. I got my arm up in time to block, then back-handed them away.

I turned my attention to the other one with a pipe and was hit on the back of the head with a glass bottle. I let the rage go. I didn't hold it back anymore.

When I came back to my senses, I watched as my attackers ran away, dragging and carrying their partners with them. I had enough. I was bleeding, I was bruised, I was uncomfortable.

Okay, fine, I was in pain. I started heading back to the lab. No one bothered me, no one came up to me. I just walked.

I was maybe a block away from the lab when I noticed the sounds of footsteps behind me. Lots of footsteps. I stopped, turned around, and saw a few dozen people headed my way.

When they saw me turn to look at them, they began yelling, cursing, and chanting at me. They called me a murderer, a beast, a monster, said it was my fault.

I knew I couldn't deal with them, so I turned back around and continued to the lab. They were still behind me when I got to the steps leading up to the doors of the facility, only now they numbered over a hundred, some of them armed.

Just as I was starting to approve of these humans, these srell destroyed it.

Where were the Xathi when you needed them?

LEENA

The entire staff was elated when Rael and I announced that we'd fixed the equation. I bet it was the best bit of news they'd gotten in months. Everyone was eager to have a part in creating the chemical mixture for the scent bombs.

I know that any scientific venture required intensive collaboration, but I never considered myself much of a team player.

I was comfortable with Rael now. I would have been happy just continuing our work together without bringing in anyone else. I didn't know if they were even qualified for this kind of work.

However, time was of the essence. It would take considerably longer to develop the stabilizing agent and incorporate it into the compound for the scent bombs with only two people working.

I let Rael choose the people she trusted most to help us. Rael stopped me as I was tugging on gloves and hunting down a pair of goggles.

"I was thinking you'd have a more supervisory role in this," she said in a gentle tone that made me almost certain she meant something else.

"I'm the most qualified," I protested, keeping my voice even. "This is why I was called out here in the first place."

"Yes, you are the most qualified," Rael agreed, though I could see the hit her pride took for her to admit that.

I almost felt bad for feeling smug. I'd worked my ass off to make headway in my field, forgive me for being excited when I was recognized.

"Which means you are the least expendable," she finished.

"Are you saying the others are?" I asked, taken aback.

Rael winced.

"Everyone here is valuable," she amended. "But we have to think long term. If our calculations were even slightly wrong and the compound became unstable, losing you would be a far deadlier blow than losing some of the others."

"And do the others know about this?" I asked, dreading the answer.

"They were eager to help! Who am I to stand in their way?" Rael said with an unsettling smile. "Watch them carefully. I don't want any accidents. It'll be up to you and me to prevent them, so we don't have to risk losing anyone."

"That's profoundly fucked up," I muttered. "Of course, I'm going to keep an eye on them. I don't want anyone getting hurt in my place."

"Then there isn't a problem," Rael said sweetly.

Rael and I closely monitored the rest of the lab staff as they tried to create the necessary stabilizing agent. So far, they were all extremely competent. I guessed that many of them were students, maybe even Rael's.

If we lived through this, each and every one of them would get one hell of a recommendation from me.

Long after I lost track of time, one of the lab techs gasped. I hurried over, convinced something had gone wrong.

"What is it? Are you hurt?" I demanded, quickly checking the tech over.

"No," she said, a smile stretching across her face. "I did it!"

"You made the stabilizing agent?" I asked, almost not believing her.

She nodded gleefully.

"Did you take notes on how you did it?"

She gestured to a notebook filled with thoroughly detailed lab work.

I grinned.

"Fantastic job. Make copies, show the others how to do it. I'll go get the casings from the engineers, and we can finally get this done!"

There was a smattering of applause and congratulations. I was still smiling when I left the lab. The engineers had been working on the physical components of the scent bomb in an old warehouse one building over.

As soon as I stepped outside, I heard shouting, angry snarls, and shrieks, too many voices to count.

I hurried in the direction of the voices. If someone was hurt, maybe I could help. I turned the corner.

A mob had formed outside the gate that surrounded the lab, the warehouse, and a few other small buildings.

Axtin was walking away from the mob. His lip was bleeding, and there were a few cuts on his green skin, but he didn't appear to be seriously injured.

At first, I felt only anger towards him, but then I heard some of the things the mob was yelling.

"Murderer!" ne of them screeched.

There were so many angry voices overlapping one another that it was hard to pick out specific words.

"Abomination."

I was running to Axtin before I could stop myself.

"Are you okay?" I asked.

He didn't meet my gaze, but he nodded.

"Alien lover!" One of the mob members hissed.

"What the hell is your problem?" I demanded.

"Things like him are my problem!" yelled one of the men at the front of the group, short and stocky with an unkempt beard and an unstable gleam in his eyes.

"It's their fault our city is destroyed. It's their fault why so many humans died. They are a blight, and we need to wipe them out!"

His deliriously impassioned speech garnered cheers from his disturbed followers.

"You idiots, he and his men saved your pathetic asses," I snapped. "The ones that did this are the gigantic crystal bugs. Even you simpletons can tell them apart."

"An alien's an alien," one of the other supporters called. "We didn't have any problems until they showed up."

"Are you serious?" I laughed, throwing my head back. "Wasn't a drug ring busted in this city last month? Pretty sure Duvest has the highest crime rate of all the settlements. And it's not like humans have never destroyed their own world before. Oh wait, we destroyed Earth. Our own planet! So, don't use my friends as a scapegoat for the fact that as a species, we were already pretty shitty!"

"I don't have to take that from an alien's whore!" The crazy-eyed man in front hissed before lobbing a rock in my direction.

His throw was pathetic. It landed three feet in front of me and five feet to the left.

"Big mistake, pal," I snarled, anger flooding my veins.

I took a step forward, preparing to grab the rock and hurl it right back at them, when I felt a strong arm close around my waist.

"Easy there, feisty boots," Axtin murmured in my ear.

I pushed against him. He was the last person I wanted to be touching me right now.

"You're a tough little thing, but you can't take on a whole mob. Let's just go before we make things worse."

"Let me go, or I'll use the rock on your pretty face," I spat.

"You think I'm pretty? How sweet of you to say," he said, slowly starting to back us up.

"Bite me," I snapped.

"You know I will," Axtin growled.

Immediately, my body flushed with heat. I opened my mouth to fire off another insult but was cut off by the sound of sirens. Four personal hovercrafts sped around the corner and halted sharply between the mob and Axtin and me.

One of them scrambled to the ground and drew his blaster. I balked when he pointed it at Axtin.

"Let the girl go and come along with us," he said.

His hand was shaking a little, and his voice lacked conviction. I doubted he'd ever fired that thing before. After the Xathi attack, I was sure a lot of the veteran officers didn't make it.

Now rookies had to step up. Great.

"Is this whole town incompetent?" I sighed, wiggling free of Axtin's grip.

Axtin lifted his hands in surrender, looking as annoyed as I felt.

"I'm *with* him, you inbreds."

"How about you don't insult the man with the blaster?" Axtin muttered to me.

I rolled my eyes at him, even though he was right.

The officer looked twitchy.

"Look," I said in a much calmer tone, "Axtin and I are working together. It's that mob you should be arresting. They attacked him. They threw rocks at me. All we are trying to do is help."

Another officer stepped up. He looked older and considerably more experienced than the one with the blaster. He looked tired.

"Ma'am, you can't blame these people for getting

riled up when you bring someone like him into the city," he explained as if I were a child.

"I brought him in so he can help me develop a weapon against the aliens that actually destroyed your lives," I hissed. "It's not my problem that those idiots are letting their baseless fears get the best of them. Axtin and his men are the reason any of you are alive right now."

The second officer pressed his fingertips into the bridge of his nose and took a deep breath.

"Look, I can't have this kind of unrest. Justified or not. I need you both to be out of the city by morning. Otherwise, it'll just get worse."

I opened my mouth to argue, but Axtin stopped me.

"Understood, officer," he said. "Leena, come on. You've got more work to do."

He gently gripped my upper arm and gave it a soft squeeze.

"Fine," I muttered, throwing one more dirty look at the mob before letting Axtin lead me back to the lab.

Once we were out of sight, I yanked my arm out of Axtin's grip.

"What the hell happened?" I demanded. "Are you sure I'm the one that needs the babysitter? It looks like you're the one who needs looking after."

Now that I was looking at him, I could see a patch of skin on his arm that looked like a chemical burn.

"I was ambushed," he said with a shrug as if it was no big deal. "A woman sounded like she was injured, I went to help her, and then the mob sprung up around me."

"You mean it was planned?" I asked.

"Definitely," Axtin muttered. "They've probably been watching us since we got here. That officer is right. It's best if we leave in the morning."

"I don't understand," I said. "All of those people survived the Xathi attack. They all saw the Xathi. Why would they think you're a threat?"

"It's normal in wartime," Axtin said dismissively. "People are scared. People are angry. They'll lash out at anything that is different, even if it's not a threat. It's an extreme method of self-preservation. They're in full survival mode now."

"No," I said. "They are using this war as an excuse to become monsters."

Without another word, I walked back into the building.

AXTIN

We left at dawn with a pack full of scent bomb prototypes. Tu'ver had run analysis on the Xathi attack patterns, and he reported a high probability that Fraga was most at risk for the next attack, after Duvest. I hoped we got there in time to help. It'd be nice to do more than pick up the pieces.

Maybe the scent bombs could work as a sort of peace offering between the humans and the *Vengeance* crew.

I didn't want a repeat of what happened with the mob in Duvest. I'm sure Leena didn't either.

I didn't expect her to defend me like that. A few days ago, she wanted nothing to do with me or any of the *Vengeance* crew. I would have thought she'd side with the humans in a heartbeat.

She surprised me. That's all that Leena did, it seemed. Surprise me.

Now she was walking beside me. She hadn't spoken since we left.

She had this look on her face like she was trying to solve a problem that either had too many solutions or none at all. It was nothing like the expression she wore when she worked.

"You okay?" I ventured.

She chewed on her bottom lip.

I wasn't sure she would answer me at all.

"It's just strange," she said after a few moments. "I keep thinking about the anger and the hate of the people that attacked you. It was like they were a different species from me."

"Are you sure?" I chuckled. "Have you seen yourself when you're angry?"

She whirled around to look at me, but she didn't look mad like I thought she would. Instead, she looked pale and fearful, like I'd just told her she was a monster. In fact, I practically did.

"Bad joke," I said with a sad smile. "You're nothing like those people. You're a little firecracker with a lot of drive and passion."

She was less sure of how to react to that, but at least she didn't look so horrified anymore.

"I am angry a lot," she murmured so softly I almost didn't hear her.

"Maybe. But it doesn't stem from a place of hatred and fear," I shrugged. "Face it, Leena. You're a good person whether you like it or not."

I definitely regretted my decision to keep our relationship professional. I was sure that was why she turned so cold to me back at the lab. Again, I was taken aback by just how little I really knew about her.

In the last two days, I'd seen her be almost mechanical in her emotional range, completely break down, reject personal connections, and crave physical connection. I didn't know who this woman was at all. And the more time I spent with her, the more I became convinced that she didn't know who she really was, either.

Or maybe everything I'd seen was just more constructed layers, and the real Leena was even farther down.

I wasn't like her. I didn't go out of my way to pick everything apart to understand all of the details and inner workings.

I was a point-and-shoot kind of guy. Give me an order, I'd follow it.

It's not my job to question things. It was my job to get this mission complete.

I knew exactly who I was. I was the muscle. I was a damn good soldier.

I'd like to think I was a pretty okay guy, too.

The chirp of a navigation unit drew me back to the here and now. Leena fumbled for something in her back pocket and pulled out a little black box. It chirped once more.

"What you got there?" I asked.

It was strange of her to be carrying her own nav unit. Jeneva had given me the one she programmed with the safest route to Duvest. I was using it now to get us to Fraga.

I didn't even know Leena had swiped one for herself. Probably to make sure I wouldn't get us lost. That seemed like something she would do.

She didn't answer me.

Instead, with her gaze still fixed on the nav unit, she made a sharp right and hurried off into the forest.

"By the systems," I grunted before rushing after her. Again with this srell? You'd think she'd have learned not to run off into the murder forest.

I couldn't see her through the thick foliage. Panic squeezed in my chest.

"Leena! Where the srell are you?"

"I'm right here. Calm down," came her reply.

I followed her voice, feeling significantly less worried and twenty times more pissed. I picked up the pace until I saw her. I grabbed her by the forearm, probably more roughly than I should have, but I needed to make sure she wouldn't run off again.

"Do not tell me to calm down," I said firmly. "You're making my job more difficult than it has to be every time you run off without a word. Do you not understand how dangerous this place is?"

She fixed me with a steely gaze. Under the weight of her cold eyes, I was tempted to apologize, even though she was clearly in the wrong.

"Of course I understand," she snapped.

She tried to wrench her arm out of my grip, but I out-muscled her. I could probably snap her arm like a toothpick. Not that I ever would.

"So, are you deliberately trying to get yourself killed?" I demanded.

"No," she scoffed.

"Are you trying to kill me, then? Believe me, female, there are better ways to do that," I continued.

She narrowed her eyes. "Can I have a list?"

Now it was my turn to scoff. "I would like to see you try," I challenged. "Seriously, what were you thinking, running off like that? I would have thought the Luurizi and the hologram trap would have been enough to curb that incredibly annoying tendency."

She flinched a little at the mention of the hologram child.

"There's something I need to pick up," she said, avoiding my gaze.

"Oh!" I exclaimed. "Is that all? Well, thank you for that incredibly informative answer. I'll just let you go about your business!"

"Your sarcasm leaves something to be desired," she said, giving me a blank stare.

"Your honesty leaves something to be desired," I fired back. "Tell me what's going on, or else I will throw you over my shoulder and carry you to Fraga kicking and screaming."

She wanted to argue. I could see it in her eyes. Eventually, logic must have won her over because she sighed.

"Fine. I need to go to a nearby Quake station," she explained.

When she didn't say anything more, I prodded.

"Full disclosure. Right now. Or over my shoulder you go," I warned.

She glared at me but kept talking.

"Quake stations are university run. I did all of my research in a university lab. All university run locations share a single data server. If I go to the Quake station, it's likely that I can recover my research," Leena explained as if it wasn't the most ridiculous thing I'd ever heard.

"You're going to risk your life, mine, and potentially

the lives of the people waiting on these prototypes for your research?" I asked.

I was sure I was missing a piece of the puzzle here.

"I'm sorry, I can't let you jeopardize the mission in this way."

In one quick movement, I scooped her up. I didn't throw her over my shoulder like I'd threatened to. She didn't struggle as much as I expected she would, either.

"This research could save Mariella's life," she blurted. "And mine," she added in a voice so quiet, I almost didn't hear her.

I immediately stopped walking and set her down. She stood facing me with her arms crossed over her chest, but there wasn't as much fight in her as there was before.

"Explain," I demanded.

"My sister and I," she began.

She paused, searching for the right words. Or talking herself up, so that she could get through it.

"We have a genetic defect. An illness. It is very rare, and, as of right now, is untreatable and incurable."

"Oh," I said, my body softening towards her. "Leena, I'm so sorry."

She didn't seem to hear me. She continued to explain in that mechanical, bare-bones way of hers.

"Our mother had it. It killed her before she turned fifty. She told us her mother had it as well, but little else. It targets white blood cells first. It makes us more susceptible to illnesses. Then it slowly shuts down organs. It's why I became a chemist in the first place. It's why Mariella became an archivist, to keep searching the records for clues. We were supposed to work together to find a cure. But one day, Mariella decided that wasn't how she wanted to spend her life. I've been working on my own ever since."

Tears glimmered in her eyes, but she refused to let them fall.

My heart broke for her. I couldn't imagine what it was like to carry the weight of something like that on her shoulders.

"Oh, Leena," I reached for her slowly, but she shifted away.

She wasn't ready to be touched yet. I understood now that she shrunk away from others when she felt vulnerable.

"That's why I am the way that I am," she said, staring intensely at a spot on the ground. "It's not fair of me to get close to people when, in a few years, I'll start showing symptoms. It's not fair to someone to have to watch me go through that with no power to stop it. And it's not fair of me to ever want children. I couldn't live with myself if I passed my cursed genetics on to a child of mine."

I'd gotten it all wrong. Leena didn't shove people

away to protect herself, she thought she was protecting others. I closed the space between us in one step and wrapped her in my arms.

She didn't resist. Instead, she let her head rest against my chest. I felt her small body shake with the sobs she'd been trying to hold in for who knows how long.

I didn't say anything, I just let her cry. I think that was all she really needed.

I kept my eyes on the forest as I ran a hand through her hair. I couldn't think of a worse time for some terrible beastie to attack.

After twenty minutes or so, Leena straightened up. She pulled away from me, but not roughly.

"Let's go," she said, her eyes still red from crying. "I've wasted enough time."

"I'm right behind you," I said with an understanding smile.

Her faint smile back was all I needed.

LEENA

Why did that keep happening?

Why was it so easy for me to walk into his arms and let him hold me? I'd never wanted anything like that before. In fact, I went to great lengths to ensure that I didn't want anything like that.

I was an idiot for telling him all of that stuff about my illness. I'd done exactly what I swore I would never do. I let my illness make me vulnerable.

The stiff feeling on my cheeks from dried tears served as a reminder that I was weak.

I thought of Mariella again. She seemed so at peace with the fact that we might never find a cure. She didn't carry the same fear I did.

Or, if she did, it didn't eat away at her as it did me. It

was entirely possible that I was wasting my life searching for a cure that couldn't be found.

But even if I made the choice to stop searching for one, I don't think I could even have just a normal life. The looming threat of the illness would weigh on my mind always.

I was grateful that Axtin didn't ask any questions about it as we walked.

He seemed content just to walk in silence.

I should say something, I really should.

Thank him, maybe? I don't know. I'd never been in this situation before. There wasn't a set procedure to follow.

In the end, I decided not to say anything.

The silence didn't last long.

We were soon approaching the Quake station. This building was part of a network that spanned a good majority of the settled world.

This planet was supposed to be a paradise, almost identical to Earth, but when the first generation arrived, that was not exactly the case. The air was breathable, and the natural food and water sources weren't toxic, but the planet frequently trembled with earthquakes. The first generation built these Quake stations to combat the issue.

Each Quake station was built around a massive drill. Each drill was perfectly placed according to the seismic wave readings received at each station. The drills basically acted like earthquake reflectors.

The quakes still hit, but these stations helped redirect them to an area far away from cities and towns. I've always wondered if that will cause problems for us in the future. Humans have many gifts, but foresight is not one of them.

From the outside of the building, the drill wasn't visible. It just looks like a very large, very square treehouse made from metal that has started to rust due to the damp, tropical climate.

It's silent. Quake stations should never be silent.

"Something isn't right," I said, looking over my shoulder at Axtin.

I was about to run in and investigate, but Axtin grabbed my arm before I could even take my first step.

"We just had a long talk about you rushing into danger and already you're looking to get yourself into trouble," he said with a grin.

I rolled my eyes but still felt a smile tugging at the corners of my mouth.

For once, I let him take the lead. He drew a blaster and motioned for me to stay behind him. We crouched low and cautiously approached the silent Quake station.

We walked up the stairs into the main building,

trying to keep our footfalls on the metal floor as silent as we could.

Axtin pressed his back against the wall beneath a window and pulled me in next to him. He lifted a finger to his lips, warning me to stay silent, as he slowly lifted himself up to look through the window.

"It's empty," he said.

"That's strange. Quake stations need to be staffed at all times," I said.

Seismic readings were constantly pouring in to be analyzed and geological experiments were frequently being performed in the Quake stations, not to mention the drill maintenance. Running the Quake station was a full-time job.

"I don't want to upset you," Axtin said hesitantly. "but a lot of the equipment and stuff isn't looking too good. I think this place was attacked."

"Xathi?" I asked, my eyes going wide in horror.

"It's hard to say. I don't see any bodies," Axtin said, taking another look through the window.

"Maybe everyone ran away?" I ventured, knowing how foolish my hopefulness sounded.

"Perhaps," Axtin said with a kind smile.

But I could see the truth in his eyes. Everyone was probably dead. From what I learned about the Xathi, they didn't just kill populations.

They harvested them.

The image of the hologram child flashed in my mind's eye. My chest tightened.

I had to stop. I had to stop thinking about it right now, or I would lose it again.

Think about your research, think about your research, I repeated to myself until I felt my heart rate slow down to a normal speed.

"Can we go inside?" I asked.

I think Axtin appreciated that I asked this time, rather than just charging in. He checked the window one more time before nodding to me. The door to the building was crumpled as if it had taken a heavy blow.

I couldn't open it. I went back to the glassless window and hoisted myself in. I heard Axtin's boots scrape against the metal floors as he followed me.

Most of the equipment was inoperable. Many of the larger machines looked like they had been smashed. Whether it was deliberate or not, I'd never know.

Crackling and sparks from some of the exposed wires told me that the power was still on. A small bit of luck in what was shaping up to be a disastrous excursion. I just needed that luck to last a little longer.

"I just need to find a working computer," I said to Axtin. "Or even a data pad. I could probably work with that."

"I don't think you're going to find one here," Axtin said, looking around the ruined facility.

With a frustrated sigh, I quickly headed toward the back of the building. In most labs, there was a designated office space with three or four computers meant for everyday work, typing up reports, submitting supply orders, and the like.

There was such a room at the back of the lab.

The first desk was missing its computer entirely. The second boasted a smashed monitor. In the farthest and least damaged corner of the room, a monitor flickered weakly.

"You any good with computers?" I called to Axtin.

He laughed and gestured to himself.

"Do I look like I've spent a lot of time working on computers?" he asked.

I couldn't help but laugh. Between the tactical armor and the insane number of weapons—especially the giant hammer—strapped to various parts of him, it was hard to imagine him sitting behind a desk typing away at something.

"Fair point," I conceded.

I approached the flickering monitor. The cable controlling the display was badly frayed. I was afraid that if I touched it, I would only make it worse.

From what I could see, the computer was still connected to the university network. The touchscreen was tricky, often not responding to my touch correctly, but I managed to open the database.

I carefully entered my credentials, having to start over several times because the monitor kept flickering out and resetting. Eventually, I was granted access to my personal database. The display was blurry and inconsistent, but it was there.

All of my research was right there where I'd left it. I could have sobbed with relief.

"It's here!" I exclaimed, beaming at Axtin. "It's all here. I snuck a data drive into the pack with the prototype bombs. Can you hand it to me?"

Axtin stared at me in disbelief.

"I don't know what's worse. The fact that you stole a data disk from a refugee lab, or that you want me to reach my hand into a bag of experimental bombs," he said.

"Just be careful, and it shouldn't be a problem," I shrugged.

The look he gave me almost made me laugh out loud.

"Or if you're too scared, just give me the bag, and I'll get it myself."

"No, I can get it," he said quickly.

He gingerly reached into the bag and pulled out the small silver data drive. He tossed it to me. I caught it and eagerly jammed it into the data port.

It took a few tries. The port was damaged. The computer didn't recognize it right away.

While I was waiting for my research to copy itself onto the data drive, Axtin spoke up.

"So, how close are you to finding a cure?" he asked.

I furrowed my brow, not sure how to answer.

"Well, that's a complicated question," I replied. "As of right now, I have the largest collection of data pertaining to this genetic disease. However, I still don't know what caused it in the first place or what could possibly be used to fight it. It's resistant to all medications used to treat illnesses with similar symptoms."

"I see," Axtin said, though I could tell he didn't fully understand.

"I'll explain it to you better when we're somewhere safe," I offered with a small smile.

"I'd like that," he grinned back at me.

Ideally, I would want to return to Duvest to work in the lab there. But I couldn't bring Axtin with me. I didn't want to risk another mob situation.

I didn't know what I would do if Axtin was seriously hurt, or worse, killed, by angry hateful humans.

Maybe I could work on the *Vengeance*. It'd be safer, and I could potentially convince Mariella to join up with me again.

And Axtin would be there. I realized with a jolt that I didn't like the idea of not having Axtin close by. But I couldn't think about that right now.

I swiped the data disk and tucked it away somewhere safe once the transfer was complete. Just having my research with me made me feel so much better.

"Let's go," Axtin suggested. "I don't want whatever caused this mess to come back looking for more."

I nodded in agreement.

We walked through the forest once again in silence. All I could think about was how I would get to the next step in my research. I was so lost in thought that I collided with Axtin's back when he stopped short.

I was about to ask him why he stopped, then I heard the shouting.

He motioned for me to get low and stay behind him. I obeyed. We worked our way through the thick trees until we came upon a small clearing.

People in dirty clothes huddled in groups as Xathi soldiers rounded them up. Some of them were children.

"Axtin," I whimpered, clutching his arm.

He put his hand over mine and squeezed.

The Xathi were wearing some kind of...suit. It didn't look like armor. They were hard as rocks, they didn't need armor in the first place. I could see energy rippling across the surface of the suits.

I was still staring at them when Axtin tried to guide me away.

"What are you doing?" I hissed.

"Leaving," he whispered back.

I dug my heels into the ground and yanked against him.

"There are children in there, Axtin!" I said, trying to keep my voice as quiet as possible.

Axtin didn't meet my gaze as he tried to move me away again.

I held fast.

If Axtin wasn't going to fight for those people, I sure as hell would.

AXTIN

Srell.

I looked at Leena and knew what the look on her face meant.

She wasn't about to leave these humans to the Xathi, and I guess, neither was I.

I had to admit though, the idea of fighting the Xathi excited me, even those wearing the power suits. If I was honest with myself, I had been itching for a fight since everything happened in Duvest.

I tensed up, ready to rush in, when Leena grabbed me by the arm and pulled me back. With her finger at her lips, she pointed off to the left. I looked back and saw three more Xathi coming, bringing more humans.

At least a dozen children, maybe more, were herded

over to the other humans. Shouts of recognition and curses resounded from where the humans were held.

I shot a look of thanks at Leena. If I had rushed in... I'm just glad she had held me back.

There were ten Xathi there, too many for me to handle on my own at the same time. The original seven would have been difficult, but I've taken down that number before.

"We need a plan," she whispered in my ear.

A small grunt of agreement was the only sound I made. I was trying to come up with exactly that.

I turned my head slightly, so she could hear my whisper.

"I'll distract them, try to draw them away from the prisoners. You take them to that small clearing we saw a mile back. If I'm not there before dusk, then get them back to Duvest."

"What about you? You can't handle that many."

There was actual concern in her voice. I liked hearing that concern, it gave me hope.

I summoned up some bravado and flashed her a "really?" look.

"And who says I can't handle that many Xathi on my own?"

"I do. You might be some alien superman, but you're not Superman. They'll kill you before I can get those people away."

"What in the name of the systems is *Superman?*"

Now it was her turn to flash me the look.

"Never mind. You can't fight ten of those things alone. But I *do* have an idea, if you're willing to listen."

I raised an eyebrow and motioned for her to continue. I turned back to watch the Xathi, but kept an ear on what she had to say.

"We have the scent bombs and some smoke grenades. Why not use them?"

It was a good idea. The scent bombs had been made specifically for this occasion, and the smoke grenades would impede their sight. They would impair our sight as well, but it wasn't a bad idea.

Before I could say anything, she reached into the pack I was carrying and brought out two of the scent bombs.

As I looked at her in shock, she smiled and threw. The two scent bombs flew, one landing between a cluster of six Xathi, the other one landing a few feet to the left.

With two consecutive "thwump" sounds, the bombs went off, spreading a pink haze into the air.

Shaking my head because I knew the pink was her decision, I watched and waited. An agonizing three seconds, which felt so much like thirty, went by before the Xathi began reacting.

Xathi soldiers are usually very disciplined thanks to

their direct connection to either a queen or a sub-queen. They didn't act on their own, they were basically an extension of a queen's own body, that's how tight and instantaneous their connection was. What I watched was a brand-new experience with these crystal bugs.

They went ballistic.

Each one started chittering and dancing around. They bumped into one another, tripped over their own legs or someone else's, one even started biting at another, trying to snap off one of the arms.

I looked over at Leena, and she was smiling from ear to glorious ear. She was happy with herself.

I was, too. She had done well.

The sense of pride that my human female had succeeded was nearly overwhelming. Then she motioned towards them while giving me the "well?" look.

I gave her a toothy grin. Battle was to commence.

And then I charged in.

This was my element.

The closest of the Xathi turned towards me—I must have let out a growl or something as I charged—and brought its six arms up to defend itself, but it was disoriented, it actually hit itself in the face with three of the limbs.

As it staggered, I shot it twice in the face with my blaster, smirking as its head cracked open.

Nine left.

Two of them started attacking each other, one fell on the ground twitching, another started digging a hole, and one began marching on the humans, causing them to shriek and scream. I took aim and fired, hitting it square in the back. It turned towards me and lunged, screaming at me as it did.

I had never heard that kind of scream before, and it hurt my brain. I fell to one knee, dropping my blaster.

I needed my blaster, but I couldn't move, couldn't think straight.

I screamed in pain, my hands pressed so hard against my head, I thought I felt something crack.

It stood over me and stopped screaming. One of its legs kicked my blaster away as it reached down and picked me up.

Through the haze, I could see that its eyes were clouded. It shook its head, then opened its mouth, spreading its mandibles out wide. It leaned in and turned its head to the side.

I punched and kicked, but it ignored my blows. As the mandibles closed around my head and started to squeeze, there was a jolt and the Xathi's body shook. It let me go and dropped me.

I was barely able to roll out of the way as the body

fell. I looked up to see another of the Xathi holding the first one's head, staring at it quizzically.

I didn't wait to see what it would do next, I grabbed one of my other blasters and emptied the clip into the thing's torso and head.

I threw my empty blaster aside, picked up my rifle—I must have dropped it when I got picked up—and started firing at anything crystal.

Seven left. No, make that six...one of them had stuck its own claw through its chest.

I emptied the clip on my rifle, reloaded, and emptied it again.

I didn't see the humans anymore, Leena must have gotten them away.

Four left. But only five bodies. One of them was missing.

My rifle clicked. I reached for another clip and realized I was out. A quick search confirmed that I had dropped them when the Xathi had picked me up.

Damn.

The mist had also dissipated. The Xathi were beginning to return to their senses. I had to end this quickly before they could broadcast back to their queen, if they hadn't already.

I unstrapped my hammer, smiled, and let out a roar as I charged. I only spent a few seconds pounding one in the back, breaking it in two.

Three.

I reached into my pouch, pulled a grenade, flipped the pin, and tossed it in the direction of one as I raced towards the other two. The "thwump" behind was all I heard.

Srell. Missed.

Not one of my better throws.

I blocked one of the Xathi's blows with the haft of my hammer, ducked under the other, and broke two of the legs of the first as I rolled between them.

With two of its three right legs broken, it fell over onto its side. It was almost comical watching it try to regain its footing, but I didn't have time to laugh. The second one came at me, with the third almost a hundred feet away.

The fight with the second one took too long. By the time I managed to get my hammer to connect with its neck, shattering it, it had already cut up my chest and cut me on the back.

Two more.

The third one, the only one still able to move capably, was wearing one of the suits...just like the one that hurt me with the scream. How in the name of all the systems had I missed that? I could see it hesitate as it seemed to take in everything.

Then it opened its mouth. Just as it started

screaming, I dropped my hammer and covered my ears. It worked, barely.

Instead of debilitating pain that drove me to my knees, it was debilitating pain that caused me to stumble.

But there was something different with this scream. It wasn't as loud, and it didn't last as long. I only felt pain for a few seconds before the scream began to lose power.

Now I just squinted due to the volume level. Finally, I understood. This one was smaller than the one that had picked me up. It wasn't a fully developed Xathi.

I smiled, showing my teeth, then charged the Xathi, grabbing my hammer as I did.

It wasn't much of a fight.

The poor thing suddenly stopped moving and looked to the sky, like it was lost. Its head turned to me and let out a small whimper as my hammer connected, sending chunks of crystalline-shell flying into the air. I kept swinging for a bit, making sure it was dead and not getting back up.

Only one more to go. I let out a little growl, and smiled my most sinister smile.

LEENA

It was hard not to watch Axtin as he dove headfirst into battle. For someone so huge, he moved with an unexpected grace as he fought. He took down that first Xathi like it was nothing. He was so in his element. So...himself. Mesmerizing. I was once again reminded of how grateful I should be that Axtin and the others were on our side. I would hate to go against him on the battlefield.

I skittered around the edge of the clearing, using the pink smoke from the grenades to my advantage. I was glad I'd gone with that color. It was harder to see through as opposed to regular smoke. And if I was going to be in the business of weapon development, I was going to stand out. Nothing wrong with a little marketing.

I forced myself to look away from Axtin. From what I'd already seen, he could clearly handle himself. I had to trust that he would do his part.

The people were being held in a pen that looked like braided and twisted wire, but wicked-looking razors punctuated each length. There were perhaps a hundred or so people in total, all trying to push themselves as far away from the Xathi as possible.

For the most part, it didn't look like anyone was seriously injured. There was a woman in the center of it all, trying her best to comfort and calm the frantic crowd without being too loud. Several children clung to her legs, though none of them looked biologically hers.

She was older than me, I think. But not very. Her sun-tanned skin glowed against her dark hair, blue eyes looking worried despite the smile fixed on her face. Quietly whispering to another person while rubbing the back of a crying child, one thing was clear. Whoever she was, she was in charge. Or, at least, she was before the Xathi showed up.

Taking advantage of the Xathi distraction, I examined the pen, frowning. If I touched it, it would slice me apart. But between two panels there was a narrow gap, maybe, just maybe enough. I slid off my overshirt and used it to tie one wire back, just a bit more.

Almost...

Maybe it was a good thing I'd been too worried to eat recently.

As it was, I barely made it through the gap before the wire cut free of the restraint, a whisper of space behind me. Quietly, I wove between the panicked throng of captives. No one noticed me except the dark haired woman.

"Who are you?" she demanded, her eyes narrowing with suspicion.

"I'm with the guy currently pounding the Xathi into the dirt," I said with a smile, trying to seem as non-threatening as possible.

"The alien," she said, looking skeptical.

"Yes. He and others are here to fight the Xathi. They rescued me and my sister when the Xathi first fell through the rift," I explained. "My name is Leena Dewitt."

"Vidia," the women said. I assumed she was purposefully leaving out her last name. "Can that alien really kill the Xathi?"

"Axtin. His name is Axtin," I said with a small smile. "And, yes, he can. He's taken down scores of those monsters. Believe me, it's good to have him on your side. If it wasn't for him, I would be dead three times over."

"You speak highly of the alien," she said, giving me a

look of appraisal. "Why were you out in the forest at a time like this?"

"We'd just come from Duvest," I explained. I wasn't sure how much I should tell her, but I needed her to trust me if I was ever going to get everyone out of here. I decided that full disclosure was the best option. "We've been working with a team to develop weapons against the Xathi. Axtin and I were delivering prototypes to Fraga when we heard screaming."

A deep sadness filled her eyes for a brief moment, then it was gone.

"Can you get them out? We've tried before, but they just keep catching us, herding us back." Vidia gestured to the panicked people around her.

"That's why Axtin's fighting," I said. "He's buying us time. I'll get the gate. You tell everyone to go as quickly and quietly to the east, where the jungle is thickest. Axtin is going to meet us when the Xathi are dead."

"He can really defeat that many?" Vidia asked, her eyes widening. If I didn't know better, I'd say she looked impressed.

"Absolutely," I beamed, hoping the doubt didn't show in my voice. Axtin was a strong, powerful, and talented warrior, but he was extremely outnumbered.

Vidia gave me a nod, and I quickly made my way back through the swarm of frightened civilians. I surveyed the pen. It had been quickly constructed from barbed wire braided together. Just touching it with my hands would tear off my flesh.

But what I did have was a surgical laser that I'd grabbed at the last minute aboard the *Vengeance*. I'd thought I'd need it for vines, not barbed wire and steel.

The laser worked just as well as if it had been used on vines. Before long, I'd weakened a section of the fencing and sliced away enough of the blades to make a small handhold. I gestured for the man next to me to hold it into place while I moved to the next joint. A small gap would slow us down, thin us out. We needed something larger. Much larger.

Vidia quickly went from person to person, whispering the plan to them. Children trailed behind her, their eyes wide and shining with fear. My heart broke for them.

One by one, more people looked to me with a sense of hope and understanding. They moved closer as I worked at the strands holding the pen together. There was a gate to the pen, but if we went through it, we would be running right into the thick of the fight between the Xathi and Axtin.

"Vidia, you've lost your mind!" A man's voice said abruptly. I quickly looked towards the clouds of pink smoke, hoping the man hadn't alerted the Xathi.

"Lower your voice this instant, you fool," Vidia hissed. She was standing toe to toe with a man several inches taller, and at least fifty pounds heavier. He looked angry, but not as angry as Vidia.

"I'm 'the fool?' You want us to go with an alien!" He was still very agitated, but, at least, he'd lowered his voice. He jabbed a finger at me. "How do you know she isn't working for them? We could be walking into a trap!"

"We're already in a trap, Anton," Vidia sighed.

"You've got to be kidding me," I muttered. I tucked the cutter away, and strode over to Vidia and the angry man, Anton.

"If you really want to take your chances with the Xathi, I'll happily leave you here," I snapped in a harsh whisper. "But I know exactly what they will do to you if you don't come with me. If the Xathi take you to their ship, you will spend the rest of your brief time on this planet wishing you'd never been born."

Anton paled several shades. Of course, I didn't know exactly what happened to humans once they were put on a Xathi ship. But I did know that those who went in never came back out. Axtin had mentioned something about the Xathi using people as resources. I didn't know exactly what that meant, but I never wanted to find out.

"Anton, do not allow your fears to put us all in greater danger," Vidia said, her voice softer, almost motherly. Anton sighed deeply, before nodding. Vidia turned to me.

"I apologize for Anton," she said. I could tell she was being genuine. "We've all been through so much, and..." I held up a hand to stop her.

"Say no more," I said. "I completely understand. It took me a while to warm up to the idea of aliens as allies as well. But Axtin and the others are here to help us." Vidia nodded.

Several people held the side of the pen in place, waiting for my signal. I looked toward the dissipating clouds of pink smoke. We didn't have much time. I was hoping for a glimpse of Axtin, but I didn't see him. I did, however, hear the sickening sound of something heavy shattering the Xathi's crystalline body. I took that as a good sign.

"On my signal," I said as loudly as I dared, "drop the fence, and run to the east. Try to stay together if you can. Be aware of your surroundings at all times." There were so many ways this could go wrong, but I forced myself not to think about it. My control over this situation was minimal. I simply had to do the best I could.

"Ready?"

They nodded.

"Go!" They dropped the fence segment, and everyone

bolted through the gap. It was chaos. Vidia secured herself a spot near the front of the stampede, so that she could direct everyone and keep them all together as best as possible. I hung back. I wanted to be the last one out. Partly to make sure everyone had a chance to escape, and partly because of Axtin. I know we agreed to meet when the dust settled, but I would feel better if he escaped with us.

A small scream from somewhere ahead of me grabbed my attention. A little girl had lost her footing and had fallen. The fleeing survivors were so panicked that not a single one stopped to help her. Most had managed to avoid stepping on her, but not everyone. The little girl curled up in a ball, paralyzed with fear. I glanced back once more looking for Axtin before dashing towards the little girl.

I shoved a fleeing adult to the side to ensure he didn't trample the child. He was in such a state that I don't think he noticed he'd been shoved. I crouched down by the little girl, and gently touched her back. Her arms were covered in small scrapes from landing hard on the forest floor. There were twigs, dead leaves, and dirt clumps caught in her long dark hair.

"You're okay, you're okay," I whispered to her. She peeked up at me, one dark eye shiny with tears. "You're going to get out of here. I promise. Okay?" She nodded. I bent down closer to her. "I need you to put your arms around my neck. Can you do that for me, little one?"

She nodded again, before raising her thin arms and wrapping them around me.

I maneuvered one of my arms under her knees, and the other around her back. "What's your name, sweetie?"

"Calixta," she whispered.

"Pretty name. Alright, Calixta, are you ready?"

She nodded once more and I lifted her and took off running. She cried quietly, but I think it was more out of fear than pain. We ran together into the thickest part of the forest. Every so often, I would catch a glimpse of another survivor running. I listened for signs of the Xathi coming after us, but didn't hear anything.

Twenty minutes passed before I found Vidia and the majority of the survivors.

"Are you missing anyone?" I asked, my lungs burning.

"A few," Vidia said grimly. "Some probably ran in the wrong direction, or ran too far."

"Hopefully, they'll find their way back to us," I said, though it sounded weak. Vidia nodded.

"What about your alien?" she asked.

"I'm going to send our location to his nav unit," I said. I thought about correcting her when she said *my alien,* but I couldn't bring myself to do it. I sort of liked the way it sounded. "Which means I've got to put you down for a second, okay?" I said gently to the little girl. She shook her head vehemently.

"A friend of mine is going to come help us," I explained. "But I have to tell him where we are first. I'll pick you right back up as soon as I do that. I promise." The little girl pulled back to look at my face. I almost gasped. At first, she looked just like the child depicted in the hologram lure. But, after the surprise wore off, I noticed several differences in the shape of her face and size. This was a different child. The other child was probably dead.

After scanning my face for a few moments, she nodded in agreement. I set her down gently. She immediately wrapped her arms around my waist and held on tightly. I smiled a little as I fished the nav unit out of my back pocket. I sent Axtin my coordinates, and picked the little girl back up.

"Now what?" Vidia asked.

"We wait," I replied.

From somewhere behind me, the plantlife snapped and rustled. Something big stalked through the forest, and it sounded like it was headed right toward us.

AXTIN

Oh, that felt good. I missed fighting. The only Xathi warrior left thrashed around on the ground, two of its legs shattered thanks to my sweetheart of a hammer. The others laughed, but this is exactly why I made her. She crushed, shattered, and destroyed almost everything she touched, and that was her entire purpose. She felt good in my hands, and the reverberation I felt when she made contact with a Xathi body brought me shivers.

I looked down at the remaining Xathi, staying just out of its reach. Even with two broken legs and unable to walk, these things were dangerous. I knelt down in front of it. It stopped thrashing around and turned its head towards me, an almost calm expression on its face.

"I know about your connection to your little queen

back home, so I know she's hearing this, or whatever it's called. If you can understand my words, then you should know that there is nothing that is going to stop me from getting you and breaking you into tiny little pieces."

The Xathi tilted its head slightly and chittered at me, almost as if it was talking *to* me.

I shook my head at it. "I don't understand your little bug noises, but I know you understand me. I'm coming for you, plain and simple."

It kept chittering at me, then made a hellish, awkward noise. It took several seconds before I realized that it was laughing at me. I stood up and smiled as my hammer crashed down onto its head, again and again until there was almost nothing left of its upper torso. Wiping blood, other fluids, and shards of shell off me, I spat on the leftovers and surveyed the scene.

There was a body missing. I searched the area. Nothing. When I looked at the tracks the refugees left behind, I noticed Xathi tracks. "Chi ko rhom ne damn dele!!!" I cursed. One had gotten away from me, and followed Leena and the others. I took off after them. I wanted to run, but I had to go at a fast walk to make sure I didn't miss the tracks and go the wrong way.

The tracks headed deeper into the trees, but away from where I had told Leena to take them. *Srell.* Where in the Abyss were they going? The Xathi's tracks were spread out, as if it was stalking the refugees. After nearly a mile, I found a body. One of the older humans must have fallen behind. He never stood a chance against the Xathi; his torso was ripped open from shoulder to hip.

I said a quick Valornian chant in his honor and continued. Two hundred yards from the body was a broken kodanos and dozens of dead talusians, more of the lethally dangerous flora and fauna of this cursed planet.

Srell. The Xathi were the only things strong enough to have broken the tree and killed that many of its swarm with ease.

I picked up the pace until, a half mile later, I found them. Only a few of the humans were there. Leena stood in front of a little girl.

A Xathi stood before them, chittering at the group.

Double srell.

The trees blocked my way, leaving only the trail for me to walk on. I was at a bad angle, it would see me coming long before I got there, and if it decided to attack Leena, it would get to her first.

Trying to be as quiet as I could, I crept closer, hoping that it would keep its attention on Leena and the little girl long enough for me to get close. It kept chittering at her, she kept cursing at it, while I kept creeping up slowly, and the other humans stood still, panicked into immobility.

The Xathi must have realized that the chittering was doing nothing, because it stepped forward with a shriek. I jumped into action, yelling out a battle cry. The Xathi ignored me and swiped at Leena, knocking her to the ground.

Everything went red. Leena was hurt, that thing stood over her, and the little girl screamed...

In an instant, I'd tackled the Xathi, knocking it away from them. I rolled off it, gained my feet, and put myself between it and them. It got to its feet, pointed at me, and started chittering. Not bothering to wait, I jumped, swinging my hammer.

I made contact with one of its shoulders with a very audible crack. It knocked me away with a shot to the chest. I blocked another swipe, ducked under a third, and rolled towards it, bringing my hammer straight up. I caught it in the chin, sending it reeling backwards. I took advantage and ducked under another swing, then swung again myself. I made contact, and continued to make contact, over and over. Everything went away.

Until Leena yelled at me, telling me it was over. I looked down in front of me, and saw that she was right...it *was* over. There was virtually nothing left of the bug, but I didn't care. I turned back towards Leena, and she was staring at me as she hugged the little girl to her. The girl was crying, and when she looked at me, she let out a little shriek and tried to get under and behind Leena.

"Shhh. It's okay. It's okay. He's a friend. He was just trying to make sure the bad bug didn't hurt us anymore." Her voice was gentle. Soothing. It made me feel something inside I wasn't sure of. Then she looked at me and flashed me that signature look of hers. "Did you really have to go crazy? What the hell is wrong with you?" She turned back to the little girl, and tried to soothe her.

I looked over at the few humans who had stuck around, and realized they were all wounded, or old. One of them came over to me. It was an older woman, and she pulled out a small piece of fabric. "You're a mess." She cleaned me up, spitting on the rag before wiping my face. Any time I tried to pull away, she glared at me, and pulled me back down to her level. I could see Leena grinning from ear to ear as she kept trying to calm the little one down.

As the woman finished up, she patted me on the chest, flashed me a small smile, and walked back, ordering one of them to get the others.

I walked over to Leena and asked. "Who's that?"

"Not completely sure, but she's definitely in charge of the group."

"That's right." We both jumped. We hadn't heard her

walk up. "My name is Vidia. I am, I mean, I *was* the mayor of Fraga. The few of us you rescued are all that's left...I think. The rest of the town was captured when the Xathi attacked this morning."

I extended my hand to her. She shook it with a solid grip. Impressive for a human. "Vidia. My name is Axtin, and this is Leena. We were on our way to you with some new weapons to fight the Xathi. I'm sorry we didn't get there in time."

She looked me up and down, visibly trying to figure me out. With a nod, she responded to my comment. "Apology accepted. You're one of those other aliens we'd heard about." It was a statement, not a question. She continued before I could respond. "From the looks of things, you've been fighting them for a while, and you look like you're fairly honest, when it matters. What do we do now?"

I thought about that for a minute. "How many are you?"

"If you're asking my age, that's a terrible touch of grammar. If you're asking how many of my people are left, I don't have an exact count; but I'm guessing it's a few dozen over a hundred. Lots of kids, lots of hurt people, too."

Leena answered. "Yeah, we saw that. That's why we stepped in when we did." She looked up at me. "Ideas?"

"There're too many wounded to make it back to

Duvest quickly, although that's probably the safer choice. We're too far away from the *Vengeance* to make it there without being attacked again. Duvest is our best choice. It'll take us about a day with the number of wounded, elderly, and children in the group."

Leena, still holding on to the little girl and singing to her quietly, looked at Vidia. "What do you think?"

"Is there anywhere for us to spend the night? No one's going to want to stay in the open for the night after what just happened. I mean, you could probably kill everything that comes at us, but I'm not sure the rest have as much faith in you as I do."

I knew I liked this woman for a reason. I smiled.

"Anyone that's crazy and stupid enough to rush into a pack of those...*things*...and come out of it alive with only a few scratches, they're okay in my book."

"Thank you, Vidia. I'll be honest, though, I'm not entirely sure if there's anything big enough for this many people," I indicated the refugees who were returning as we spoke. "At least, none that I know of, butI am relatively new to this world of yours."

"That's an understatement."

Leena put up her hand. "Hi. Still here if you two want to hear my ideas."

With a chuckle, I nodded in apology. Vidia smiled and took a half-step back, motioning Leena to continue.

With a quick roll of the eyes, Leena told the little girl, again, that I was a good guy, then looked at us. "I know of a place we can go…it's big enough for all of us, and if our hero here doesn't mind a little bit of heavy lifting, it's easy to close up so we'll be safe." She smiled at me when she said 'hero'. I smiled her a promise back.

Vidia chuckled at us, muttering something about hormones, as she turned to look at her people.

LEENA

It was just as I remembered it, even years after I'd last stepped foot in the place. I turned to Axtin as we came to the small cave entrance, already prepared for the questioning look on his face.

My place of solitude that I had discovered when I was younger. The cave was lit by naturally bioluminescent moss, and had been my refuge when the world had seemed too overwhelming to a young girl.

And now it was being used to give me shelter from the world once more.

"It's bigger than it looks," I said, "trust me."

He nodded once, fully willing to take me at my word, it seemed.

"You lead the way."

I waited until I was facing away from him to let the small smile spread across my face. I knew it wasn't the right emotion to feel at such a time, such a place, but I couldn't help myself. I knew what he was up to.

If asked, he'd probably have just said that I knew the place, it made sense for me to go ahead of him. But I wasn't born yesterday. He was keeping an eye on me, always looking out for me.

It might have been wrong to smile after what all these people had been through, but his concern was starting to grow on me. *He* was starting to grow on me.

I led the group through the opening, a light clutched tightly in one hand. I hadn't been to these tunnels since I was at university. It soon became clear, though, that they hadn't changed a bit. Same twists, same turns. Count on Mother Nature to remain constant even as the whole world goes to hell.

From somewhere in the distance, I heard the familiar patter of dripping water, the soft echo of our footsteps. It was surreal to be back after so long, not to mention after so much change.

If someone told me back at university that I would one day lead a group of alien-attack survivors into this place, I would have laughed my ass off. Well, more likely, I would have declared them insane, and gone right back to studying; but, same idea.

I forced my mind back to the present, turning as best I could to Axtin.

"There's a larger space up a ways, big enough for everyone."

He nodded, turning back behind him to pass on the information.

It was only another minute or two before the tunnel began to widen. Soon after, we found ourselves in a wide chamber. The ceiling was high, twenty feet, at least, and practically dripping with stalactites.

Everyone piled into the space, immediately filing to the center. After being trapped in a cage and then forced to walk through narrow tunnels, I had expected everyone to spread out, but they didn't. Instead, they stood close, huddled together as if for warmth. Few of them spoke and those who did spoke in the barest of whispers, their tones hushed and heavy with fear. Calixta wiggled out of my arms to go to some of the other children, and my heart ached a little, thinking of what she must have lost in the past day.

I knew I should say something, offer some kind of comfort, but words seemed to fail me. What could I possibly say to people who had just been through so much? Moreover, why would they even listen?

Still, I opened my mouth, willing the right words to come. Or any words for that matter.

I was spared the effort in the next moment as a voice rose from the center of the crowd.

"Alright, everyone, it's okay. We're safe now."

Vidia, of course. I breathed a sigh of relief.

Heads swiveled in her direction, all eyes immediately locking on the older woman.

"I know we've all been through something tonight, some worse than others. But if we keep our heads straight, we can all come through this. What we need to do now is take stock. Food, water, whatever we've got on us, let's see it. We need to know how long we can stay here."

"Excellent idea," Axtin said, stepping forward. "We'll all feel much better once we have a solid plan."

Everyone sprang into action at Vidia's command, idle hands springing to life, each grasping to produce what little they had.

Moments later, Vidia, Axtin, and I crouched near a small pile of goods. Small being the operative word. All told, there was just enough food to get us through the night, possibly enough water.

We were safe, that was the most important thing, but without food and medical supplies, we wouldn't stay so for long. We needed a plan, and we needed one fast.

"What are we going to do?" I asked, directing the question to both of them at once.

Vidia gazed around at the shaken people, her brows knit as she thought.

"I might have an idea," Axtin offered, standing by my side. "Vidia, can you get everyone settled while we talk?" She nodded once, immediately standing to see to her task. He reached down, taking my hand, "Come with me."

For someone who had never stepped foot in the place before, he seemed to navigate the tunnels quite well. In no time at all, he had led me deep into the heart of the labyrinth, coming to a stop in a particularly wide passageway.

"Okay," I said, pulling my hand from his grip. "What's the plan?"

"You're not going to like it."

I scoffed, rolling my eyes pointlessly in the near dark.

"Just tell me."

"I need to leave for a while, go back to the *Vengeance.*"

My heart seemed to stutter in my chest.

"*Leave?*" I managed, feeling suddenly panicked all over again.

"Just for a while. To get help."

It made sense, I knew immediately that it did. But, somehow, I still felt like the air had been knocked from my lungs.

"I don't know, Axtin…"

"Leena," he said, his voice oddly calm. "We can't bring them all with us right now. You know as well as I do that a lot of them wouldn't survive the trip through the forest. They're wounded, some of them are children. If I go alone, I can bring back food, supplies, even guards. It's the only way we stand a chance at saving them all."

"I could go with you." I said, the words sounding hollow even to me.

"You could. I just assumed you'd want to stay and help here."

I did. Or, some part of me did, anyway. The rest of me was still flooding with that sense of panic, of breathlessness. The thought of Axtin leaving made me feel ill and helpless.

I nodded anyway, "You're right, I do."

"I can travel faster alone, anyway," he said, taking a step nearer in the already cramped tunnel. "I'll be back before you know it."

I nodded again, or maybe I had never stopped. Either way, I knew it was the right thing to do. I tried not to focus on the pit in my stomach, on the strange desire I felt to beg him to stay. It was wrong to want him there when he could help so many people by leaving. So I nodded, my hair bouncing around my head with the intensity of my agreement.

Truth be told, I was afraid. That something would happen to him, that he wouldn't make it back. I knew better than to voice the thought. Still, my hands trembled as I faced him.

"It's a good plan."

He smiled down at me, his eyes sparkling sadly in the dim tunnel.

"I'm coming back."

"I know." My voice was unconvincing, even to me.

I felt his hands on mine then, the gentle pressure drawing me more presently to the moment.

He stared down at me, his gaze penetrating.

"I *am* going to come back, Leena." His words were slower, more definite.

I met his gaze, biting my lip in concentration.

"I know you will."

"Leena—"

I couldn't hear anymore, couldn't think anymore. It was too much: the Xathi, the wounded, him leaving. My heart felt like it might burst from the strain.

Whatever he was going to say, it didn't matter. There was nothing *to* say. He had to leave, and I had to stay behind. There wasn't any other option, and we both knew it.

For the time being though, he was still there, still with me. And I could no longer bear the thought of not touching him.

I rose quickly to my toes, sipping at his lips.

He responded immediately, his hands finding my waist to pull me tighter against him. His tongue pressed against my own, the taste of him sending waves of electricity through me.

I moaned into his mouth, my own hands scrambling over him. I wanted to feel him, every solid inch of his body. My fingers slid into his shirt, over his abs, around his back. He felt better than I ever imagined, greater than any fantasy.

His cock throbbed between us, the press of it feeling enormous, even through our clothes. It was rigid, in a way that my brain exploded just thinking about.

He took my lip between his teeth, biting down so that I groaned in pleasure. I had never known, before Axtin, just how good pain could be. I gripped him in response, my nails biting into his back until a growl escaped him. Even that, the mere sound of him, made me wild.

I reached for his shirt, needing more of him, wanting to see him. It pulled easily over his head and he answered in kind, tearing at my clothes like a madman. In no time at all, we were free of them, and they lay littered across the tunnel, some having ripped in our mad rush.

When we were finally bare, we paused, taking a

moment to see one another; really see, for the first time.

Axtin may have been the single most amazing thing I had ever seen. He hulked over me, looking even larger than normal in the narrow tunnel. His green skin stretched tightly over perfectly sculpted muscle, his chest heaving in excitement. I lowered my eyes slowly, taking in his full glory while my heart pounded in my chest.

His cock was enormous, bigger than I had thought possible. The mere sight of him, hard and throbbing, made my breath catch in my throat. I had never wanted anyone as badly as I wanted him in that moment. All of him. Every solid inch.

He was soon to accommodate.

He reached for me in the next moment, pulling me against him as his hands continued their exploration of my body.

Sparks ran through me as one finger grazed my swollen lips, taunting me with his nearness.

"Almost, just a little higher," I whispered, then shuddered as he teased over my clit.

"What was that, sweetheart?" he breathed into my ear. "Should I do that again?"

I nodded, not trusting my voice. Hell, I wasn't sure I could make complete sentences anymore.

Pressed against his shoulder, I moaned into his chest

as he strummed across my clit with his thumb, alternating with faster strokes of his fingers against my slick folds.

My knees buckled, but he held me, refused to release me against the storm of sensation.

"So tight, Leena," he muttered as one thick finger pushed inside me. He pumped, added another finger, stretching me further. "So perfect."

I squeezed my eyes shut, just to focus on that delicious feeling.

"Eyes open," he commanded. "I need to see you, see all of you."

My head lolled back as he pierced me with the heat of his gaze.

Yet another finger teased my opening, spiking the intensity until I panted. "What are you..." Nope, no coherent sentences from me.

He dropped kisses down my neck, pressed into me again. "You're too tiny," his ragged breathing matching my own. "But I have to have you." A muscle in his jaw twitched. "Can't hurt you."

A final pump and twist of the fingers deep inside me and I came apart on his hand.

Before the waves stopped, he spun me, turning me so that I faced the tunnel wall. His teeth danced on my shoulders, my back. Pain flared through me, sparks of pure ecstasy the likes of which I'd never known.

And he was just getting started.

His fingers reclaimed my clit as he positioned himself behind me. I braced myself, leaning my weight against the cool stone of the tunnel, fingers spread as he began to push his way inside me.

Inch after throbbing inch he slid into me, filling me completely.

He paused, kissed my back. "Alright?" I nodded, flexing my knees to rock back against him when I realized.

He wasn't done.

By the time he was halfway in, he'd had to muffle my moans of pleasure with his other hand, both of us anxious not to have unwanted company investigating my cries.

And still, he pressed forward. I thrust back in answer, desperately needing to feel all of him. After another moment, I finally did. He was like nothing I had ever experienced before, my vision blurred in pleasure.

"Leena," he groaned, "srell!"

I shoved against him, driving him ever deeper into my pussy until his hard thighs pressed against the back of my legs.

We both panted while I adjusted to the feel of him. In me, over me, his hands caressing even while he nipped my skin. Axtin's touch became everything.

And then he started moving. Slowly, gently, relentlessly pistoning with iron control.

My fingers scrambled against the cave wall, nails sliding over the rough stone as he drove into me. His hands at my back, his teeth resuming their work on my shoulders, my neck.

It was too much, all of it so profoundly overwhelming, I felt I might burst. And, still, I wanted more. *Needed* more.

"Axtin, please," I whimpered, not even sure what I begged him for.

His iron control snapped, strong fingers digging into one hip as he hammered into me like a wild man, faster and harder until I started to fly, inundated by sensation.

Electricity shot through me, pooling in my center, building as I ground myself against him.

I felt his fingers in my hair, twining and pulling until my head wrenched backward, more of that amazing pain working its way through my scalp. It was all I could take, the last on a list of indescribable pleasures.

Deep inside me, his cock grew, swelled until, with a shuddering pulse, he came, his shout more a roar.

Too much, too intense. Too everything.

"Axtin!" I screamed, the word a prayer as my orgasm tore through me, leaving me shivering in his arms.

AXTIN

I can't say I was happy to go. If anything, finally getting to be with Leena was only making it more difficult. As I wound my way back through the tunnels, though, it was like a weight had been lifted from me.

Leena and I could make this work. I knew that now. It wouldn't be easy, but, then again, nothing worth doing ever was. And I was certain now that this was. Leena was worth all the trouble it would cause, and then some.

Still, I hated to go. I knew there was no other choice, these people would all die if we couldn't get them supplies soon, but the thought of leaving Leena worried me. What if something happened while I was away? She and the rest of the survivors weren't exactly up to the task of fighting off the Xathi.

I ran a hand through my hair, pondering imaginary options for one more time since having left Leena. There was no other way, no good answer. I had to go, and she had to stay.

I pushed my worry to the back of my mind as I threw my pack over my shoulder. There was nothing to be done for it. Worrying wouldn't help.

The sooner I left, the sooner I could return, this time bringing supplies and safety with me. It was worth the risk.

I didn't bother saying goodbye to anyone as I made my way towards the exit. Leena and I had already said our goodbyes in the tunnels, and I was fairly certain that no one else would care to hear it from me. I still sensed their distrust, it was heavy in their gazes, in the way they moved aside whenever I neared them.

Given time, I hoped they would come to accept my presence, but I wasn't exactly counting on it. Either way, I wasn't about to stress. The only human whose opinion I valued was Leena, and I now had a pretty good idea of how she felt about me.

The night was falling as I finally made my way from the cave, only dim light now making it through the trees. It was going to be a long night, walking back to the *Vengeance* alone. With a sigh, I started forward.

The forest was deceptively quiet, giving the impression that I was alone in the growing dark. I had been on this planet long enough to see through the illusion, of course, but it was odd to step into such silence after the cramped quarters of the tunnels.

Humans are loud, even when they try not to be. There's always some sound giving away their location: a rustle, a sigh, even their breathing seems loud. In a way, it was nice to be back in the silence.

I walked for a long while, thinking of Leena and our time together as I went. She had surprised me, once again, back in the tunnels. I smiled, pulling my pack tighter on my shoulders. I would probably never have a dull moment with that one, but, srell, I no longer thought I wanted any.

Leena had been a surprise since the first moment I'd laid eyes on her, and I didn't think she was going to stop being one any time soon.

After another few moments of thought, I was off again, heading quickly in the direction of the *Vengeance*.

It was easy to daydream, there was no denying that, but I had someplace to be, someone to take care of, and I didn't want to stick around and risk another attack.

Who knew what might come next? Judging from what I'd seen so far, it could be anything.

It occurred to me that Jeneva should really teach those of us from the *Vengeance* how to handle the local wildlife. Traversing by oneself was risky at its best. Had we better knowledge, we could have brought the refugees over all at once. If anyone could be called an expert on such things, it would be her. After all, she did live among all the monsters for years.

I smiled, thinking of her, of *them*, really. Jeneva and Vrehx were lucky to have found each other. I wouldn't have thought it possible to begin with, but they were actually a perfect fit.

Jeneva had changed remarkably since we met her. She was no longer the same stoic woman who we found in a cave. In fact, she had become almost friendly. And Vrehx, well, Vrehx no longer lived as if his sole purpose was to maintain order, a fact for which we were all deeply grateful.

It made me hopeful, knowing that two such different people were making it work. After all, if Jeneva and Vrehx could pull it off, things would likely be just as easy for Leena and me.

I had gotten so lost in thought, I almost didn't notice when I finally approached the *Vengeance*. The trip back wasn't nearly as long as I'd imagined. I smiled as I approached the door, feeling like I was coming home after a particularly bad day.

A moment later, I was back inside the ship proper, saying quick hellos as I searched for General Rouhr. I found him in the hall, looking half-relieved to see me.

"General."

"Axtin, how did it go?" he asked me.

After all that had happened, it took me a moment to remember why we had even left to begin with.

"Oh, very well, General," I said. "Leena was successful with the scent bombs."

"Ah, finally, good news," he sighed.

"Well, I wish that was all that happened. We had a run-in, sir, with the Xathi."

He seemed to finally notice I was alone, looking over my shoulder in question.

"Leena?" he asked.

"Fine, she's fine. But she and a group of survivors are hiding near Duvest, running very low on supplies."

He furrowed his brow in thought.

"Near Duvest, you say?"

"That's right."

"Where exactly?"

I resisted the urge to rush him to action, knowing I'd get nowhere without answering his questions.

"They're in a tunnel system between Fraga and Duvest. Sir, there are nearly a hundred survivors, many injured, some children. They need supplies and guards immediately. I'll organize it."

I turned to go, content to let him think it through while I spread the word.

"Axtin," he said.

I suppressed a growl, turning back to him.

"Yes?"

"Engineer Thribb has been testing short-range satellites."

I was practically thrumming with impatience, but his words stilled me.

"And?"

"A Xathi horde has been spotted in the vicinity"

I didn't wait to hear more. I couldn't. Before he'd even finished his sentence, I was off, rushing to gather the men.

LEENA

I watched the canteen pass between sets of tiny hands, each child taking a small drink before passing it to the next. They didn't complain, which, in some ways, was worse than if they did.

How quickly they had adjusted to this new reality, how deeply they seemed to understand the dire straits we had found ourselves in.

I kept the smile plastered on my face as the container made its way back to me, now almost empty. It wouldn't have done any good to show them my concern. They had already developed enough worry themselves.

"When will the green man be back?" a little boy asked, excitement touching his features.

They were so small. Their minds were not yet

plagued by the prejudices of their elders. In fact, most of them seemed downright fascinated, rather than afraid, by Axtin.

"Very soon."

"Good," he answered, sounding serious. "I like his hammer."

My laughter was genuine as I reached across to ruffle his hair. Of all the things to mention.

"Well, he and his hammer will be back before you know it," I replied.

They all smiled at that, hope shining through their dirt-smudged faces. I tucked the canteen into my belt and stood, saving the last bits of water for later.

"You all play nice now," I said. "I'm going to go check on the grownups."

It already seemed like a long time since Axtin had left. My nerves were completely fried in his absence. I had gotten so used to having him around. I felt almost vulnerable without him at my side.

Despite that, though, I still knew he had made the right choice. Leaving wasn't easy for him, but it was our only chance. All I had to do to remind myself of that fact was look at the children running around the tunnels.

And believe me, I was needing a lot of reminding.

I had barely made it half way across the space when

I felt a tug at my hand. I knew without looking who it was.

"Calixta," I said, turning with a smile. "Don't you want to play with the other kids? Maybe with Koda? He looks lonely."

She looked offended at the suggestion, tightening her grip on my hand as she gazed up at me.

She had hardly left my side since I got back to the main cavern after Axtin's departure. Not that I could blame her.

After our little run-in with the Xathi, I think I was the only person she truly trusted. She clung to me as she had in the forest, as if her life depended on it.

I had asked Vidia about her parents and learned that they hadn't survived the attack. She was all alone here.

"Alright then, if you're sure," I said.

"I'm sure, Leena." She smiled, her entire face lighting up.

It was all I could do not to cry.

"Okay, I'm just going to be checking on people, boring stuff really," I said.

"I don't mind," she replied.

"Suit yourself," I said with a smile.

But I was happy for the company.

I set my sights on a group of people huddled on the other side of the cavern. Some of them looked a little worse for wear. Most of the badly wounded were still lying off to the side, but some of the others weren't in much better shape.

"How are we doing?" I asked as we approached, resuming my phony smile.

Several sets of eyes swiveled to meet me, varying levels of weariness seeming to radiate from them.

"We're low on water," one woman offered, gesturing towards a canteen at her belt. "And we need medical supplies quickly."

I knew that most of the containers in the tunnels were in similar condition, the townspeople not having had much on them to begin with.

"The water here is safe to drink. As far as supplies, we're working on fixing that as soon as possible."

"When the alien returns, you mean?" a skeptical-looking man asked.

"Yes, that's what I mean," I said with steel in my voice.

He had the nerve to scoff, his eyes rolling in his too small head as he did so.

"I realize that everyone's worried," I started, trying to keep the irritation from my voice. "But Axtin will be back soon with food and water."

"And if he doesn't?" the first woman asked.

It was all I could do not to growl. "He will."

The group exchanged looks of disbelief, their concern obvious.

"I know you think that," the man said, taking a step nearer to us. "But the rest of us aren't so sure. He's an *alien,* for fuck's sake. He doesn't have any loyalty to us humans."

"Is that so?" My voice hardened, taking on its familiar edge. "If you have a better solution, I'm sure we'd all love to hear it."

He lowered his head, grumbling unintelligibly.

"I'm sorry," I said. "What was that?"

"Look," he said, raising his eyes to meet mine. "Just because you trust that thing doesn't mean he hasn't left us to die."

I glanced down at Calixta, if only to remind myself that she was still present. With her there, my options for rebuttal were limited.

I couldn't, for example, rip the man's head from his shoulders and use it as a ball, as much as I might like to.

"Okay, I'm getting a little tired of your mouth," I said instead. "So let's be clear here. That *thing* as you call him, is your one and only chance of making it through this alive. If you want to doubt him, I can't stop you. But given that you have literally no other options, you might as well trust him."

I didn't wait for a response. What would be the point?

I turned away from the group, hoping but not really

believing, that my words might have some effect on them.

They made me feel ashamed. Of my species, for one, but mainly of myself. I couldn't listen to their inane fears without remembering that I myself had voiced similar thoughts.

It wasn't their fault, I told myself. It was natural to fear the unknown. The thoughts did nothing to quell my anger.

Natural or not, it was wrong.

All Axtin had done since crashing on this godforsaken planet was try to help. And still, he was met with nothing but fear and distrust, if not outright hatred.

It made me sick.

"Are you okay?" Calixta asked, her words tinged with worry.

I had to remind myself again that she was still with me, that I couldn't fall apart. Not yet anyway, for her sake if nothing else.

"I'm fine, sweetie," I said. "Let's just go sit down."

She nodded as she followed me over to a blessedly empty spot along the wall.

We sat in comfortable silence as Calixta used a loose stone to draw on the rocky ground, while I dug desperately through the same old thoughts.

I worried that something would happen to Axtin. I

worried that even if he got here, it still wouldn't be enough. Fear and doubt spun through my mind on an endless loop, harsh and unrelenting.

I leaned against the wall, closing my eyes and trying my best to shut out the worry. It served no purpose, would help nothing.

For a long time I sat motionless, letting the exhaustion lull me into a though-less state. I hadn't even realized just how tired I was until I had stopped moving.

The space around me grew steadily quieter as everyone relaxed, the conversations slowing and eventually dropping off. It was odd, considering how much had happened, but there really wasn't much to say.

There were no solutions to discuss nor plans of action. At some point the rest of them must have figured it out because by the time I opened my eyes again, I was surrounded by silence.

I glanced over at Calixta, realizing she had wandered off to Koda at some point. The two of them were now sleeping with their heads together. The rock she was using to draw was still cradled in one tiny fist, her expression peaceful in the safety of sleep. I grinned down at her. Even though we'd only just met, I had already grown fond of her.

I lay beside her, letting myself drift off in the dim

lighting. I don't know how long I slept. Not long enough, that much is for sure.

I woke with a start. Something must have drawn me from an admittedly fitful sleep.

It was a sound, far off but persistent. Something grating, a scraping. My mind lazily spun back to Calixta and for a moment I thought she might have woken up and started her makeshift drawing again.

It made enough sense that I almost accepted it as fact and went back to sleep, but something stopped me.

With a groan I rose onto my elbows, looking around through sleep-addled eyes. Calixta was just where I'd seen her last, still sleeping soundly at my side.

Something was wrong.

I sat upright and examined the space for movement as I tried my hardest to identify the sound. It was growing louder, that much was for sure, an insistent scraping that I couldn't quite place.

I stood, walking to the nearest tunnel, my head craned towards the sound. It was definitely coming from the tunnel. Chills ran down my spine, my hair standing on end.

I could hear it in the tunnel, could sense it coming closer. But it wasn't only there. The sound was coming from behind me as well.

I spun, panic rising in my chest. No, not just behind me, it was coming from all sides.

It finally clicked the moment before they came pouring in.

Legs. What I was hearing was the sound of legs scraping against the rough stone of the tunnels. Not human, of course, but the crystalline limbs of the Xathi.

"Calixta!" I screamed, sprinting back towards the sleeping child.

But it was too late.

From all around us, from several tunnels at once, the Xathi flooded into our clearing, the hair-raising grating sound seeming to rise in crescendo as they came.

We were completely surrounded.

AXTIN

I found Vrehx and our team in the cafeteria, grabbing a bite to eat. "Commander!"

Vrehx looked up from his meal and swallowed his bite before answering. "You made it back. Karzin and his team had a pool started on whether or not you'd return. I…"

I didn't let him finish. "Sir, I just found out from Rouhr that a Xathi horde was spotted just a bit out of Duvest."

"That's right."

"Leena's in that area. As are a bunch of wounded refugees and children."

"Srell!" He turned to the rest of the team and issued orders. "Get your gear, we're out in two minutes."

The others nodded and left without question.

"If it's a horde, we need more guns." I needed to reload anyway.

"I'm not going to stop you from loading up, you know that," Vrehx said to me, speaking slowly.

"Not what I meant," I corrected myself, speaking slowly. "We need another team. They're starting to use the suits."

"Shit!"

I looked at him with a thin grin on my face. "Excuse me?"

He shook his head and chuckled as he opened the armory doors. "Been around the humans too much. Starting to pick up their language."

"I understand that. These humans are intriguing."

"They are, indeed," Vrehx agreed with a chuckle.

The team laughed as they finished loading up. Then Vrehx looked at me and shook his head. "Turn around and take the straps off."

"I don't follow"

Vrehx sighed. "You're bleeding all over my armory. Turn around so I can hit you with the med-foam," he said to me. "You're useless dead."

It was my turn to sigh, but I did as ordered. I turned around and took off my hammer.

As Vrehx sprayed my wounds with the med-foam, a fantastic invention by Zairk and our medic, he told Tu'ver to go get Karzin and his team and have them catch up. He finished spraying my wounds, which stung *just* a little, but I was grateful.

I gave him a nod, then re-strapped my pack and put my hammer backinto its harness.

"The suits are a problem, however," Vrehx said finally. "The queens must have decided to conserve their soldiers, send out weaker castes to fight."

I nodded. It made sense. The Xathi were making use of every tool they had. Just as we needed to do. And for all we knew, they could make more suits faster than they could hatch more soldiers.

I grabbed a few more blasters, another pack of grenades, and headed out the door. I led the way, Vrehx and Daxion to my left, Sakev to my right, and Tu'ver bringing up the rear.

We made our way north at a healthy jog, Karzin and his team a few hundred yards behind us.

When we arrived at the Quake station, we turned a bit west. We were close. I kept a look out, hoping we would see the Xathi tracks heading away from the tunnels, and only slightly hoping we'd run into them first.

I was itching for another fight against those bastards.

We weren't that lucky. The Xathi tracks were all over the entrance of the cave, too many of them going inside. I let out a very human string of curses and entered the tunnels.

Tu'ver took Rokul and Takar down one branch, Vrehx and Karzin went down another, Iq'her went down a third branch with Sylor and Sakev, leaving Daxion to try and keep up with me.

I knew the tunnels were empty.

There was no way they could have hidden that many people that well, or that quietly. The Xathi had them, I knew they did, but I tried to hold out hope. I didn't try for long. The tunnels were empty.

Srell! The damn bugs had Leena. Had the one thing I truly wanted in this life.

I used the comms to call everyone back to the cave entrance.

"We need to go after them." I fought to keep my calm as I paced back and forth.

Tu'ver examined the tracks, trying to separate the chaos from the questions.

Vrehx put his hand on my shoulder as he came up behind me. "We came out prepared for a quick strike and retrieval. Not this."

I threw his hand off my shoulder and turned on him. "What in the name of *everything* are you saying? We're not going after them?"

"The longer we're away, the more we're putting the entire ship in danger." He scowled. "You know that."

"I don't give a shit," I borrowed from Leena's

extensive cursing repertoire. "We can't leave these people to the damn Xathi. We need to save them. Even if we don't have room for them on *Vengeance*, we can escort them to Duvest."

I was losing my temper. The only reason that I hadn't punched this sanctimonious-rule-following-srell in his pretentious little jaw was that I needed him. I couldn't rescue Leena and the others by myself.

I needed all of them.

Then Vrehx opened his mouth and said the wrong thing. "No, I'm calling this mission off. We don't know what we're walking into. We don't know how many Xathi are involved right now, or even where they took the humans."

Tu'ver spoke, "I know where."

I don't think I've ever seen Vrehx jump like that. I just wished I could make fun of him for it later, but I jumped about as high as he did.

Vrehx cursed a bit in his language as he started taking in deep breaths. "Damn it, Tu'ver. Stop sneaking around. And what do you mean you know where?"

"I know where, or at least, I know what direction. They headed east, towards Nyheim."

"That's where they crash landed. They're heading back to their ship."

"Then we know where to go," I said.

Vrehx shook his head again. "That makes it even

worse. They headed back to their ship where the *rest* of them are. Hell, by the time we get there, the humans might not even be alive anymore."

"I don't give a fuck. I'm going, with or without you," I said slowly, not mincing my words.

"No, you're not!" he yelled at me. "I'm giving you a direct order, soldier."

I lost it. "Screw you and your damn orders! I'm going after them!"

"Don't make me arrest you, Axtin," Vrehx snapped. "I swear I will."

"Take yourself to the Abyss. If this was Jeneva, you'd be going after her, but because it's Leena and you don't have a vested interest in her, she can just die?"

I was in his face, bearing down on him. "You're honestly about to tell me that you're allowed to sleep with a human and be happy, but if the rest of us find a mate, we can't have them?"

He opened his mouth to say something, but I put my hand on his face and pushed.

"You can accuse me of desertion, you can hunt me down, you can try whatever you want, but I'm going to get Leena and the rest of them and I don't really give a *shit* what your thoughts on that are."

I hoped, so badly, I hoped he would attack me. I wanted to wipe that damn look off his face.

"You ever touch me like that again, I'll break you," he snarled, but didn't move.

"So be it. I'm getting my mate back and I don't give a srell what you say." I walked off, heading towards Nyhiem and the Xathi ship.

I heard Vrehx and the others fall in behind me, Karzin talking to Vrehx in hushed tones. If they were planning my court martial, I didn't care. I didn't give a damn about that anymore. My only thoughts were on Leena and breaking every damn Xathi I could get my hands on.

The brothers, Rokul and Takar, came up beside me. Rokul was the one that spoke. "So, you've taken a human female. How is she?"

I growled at them both and increased my pace, trying to leave them behind. They kept up with me.

"Our apologies, we did not mean to offend," Takar said. "We merely wanted to ascertain if being with a human female was worth the effort or not." He was always formal when he spoke, even when he was being an asshole.

"You two are ridiculous. Get away from me."

They retreated a few steps but stayed close by. I don't know if they were ordered to stay close or if they decided to on their own. Frankly, it didn't matter. In a crazed way, I was pleased. They gave me something extra to throw if anything tried to attack.

LEENA

The Xathi herded us into a dark and cold room, with floors out of some sort of metal that sucked the warmth from us the moment our skin made contact.

I kept a tight hold of Calixta's hand as the heavy door slammed shut behind us. I heard a thunk as the locking mechanism slid into place.

The only light came from a series of glass panels on one side of the room. On the other side was a room of some sort filled with equipment I didn't recognize. I didn't want to know what it was for.

Beside me, Calixta whimpered.

"Hey," I said softly, crouching down beside her. "We're okay."

She leaned into me, hiding her face in the crook of my neck.

"I don't like the dark," she cried. I rubbed her back in small circles.

"That's okay," I said, trying to keep my voice bright. "I don't like the dark either! Let's try to be brave together, okay?"

Calixta sniffled and nodded, wiping at her tears.

"Is Koda here?"

"I'm sure he is!" I smiled, even though the answer to the question made me sick to my stomach. "Let's go find him, okay? You know, sometimes the dark can be really scary but it's also really good for playing make-believe. Maybe you and Koda can think of a fun game to play!"

The idea appealed to Calixta. She nodded and excitedly began to look for her friend.

I didn't want to think about what I would tell her if she couldn't find him.

When she found Koda, she let go of my hand to hug him. I chewed on my bottom lip, trying not to cry.

"How about you two play for a bit while I talk to some of the grown-ups? But play quietly, though, okay?" I asked, trying not to look nervous.

"We'll be quiet so the monsters don't come," Calixta said with a somber nod.

I was truly amazed at how much she and the other

children understood. But at the same time, I was immensely relieved they couldn't grasp the full reality of our situation.

"Let's build a big laser so we can help the green man kill all the monsters!" Koda whispered excitedly.

I couldn't help but smile. If...no...*when* I saw Axtin again, I think it would make him happy to know how much these kids looked up to him.

Leaving the kids to play, I found Vidia standing by one of the glass panels, her arms wrapped around her body. She was staring intently at the various machines on the other side of the glass.

"What do you think they're for?"

"I'm trying not to think about it," I said bleakly.

"Will your friends come for us?" she asked as she turned to look at me. Her face was drawn. She looked like she hadn't slept in weeks.

I'm sure I didn't look any better.

"Of course," I said with confidence. "Axtin wouldn't just leave us here to—" I couldn't bring myself to say the word 'die'. I wasn't going to let myself go there.

Axtin was probably on his way right now.

"Those...things took all of our equipment," Vidia spat angrily. "The radios, the nav units, everything! What do they even need it for? How is your friend going to find us if you don't have your nav unit?"

"The Xathi are too big to move stealthily through

the forest," I said as calmly as I could manage. "A hundred or so people aren't subtle either. We would have left a clear trail behind us. Axtin and the others will have no problem following it right to the ship."

"You have a lot of faith in him," Vidia mused.

"What's the alternative?" I replied.

Before Vidia could answer, the door we had been herded through slid open with a loud bang. Two Xathi, one black and one blue, stood in the doorway. They clicked and chirped to each other.

For some reason, the fact that they had a language disturbed me even more. Because of their appearance, it was easy for me to categorize them as animals that killed because it was their nature. But no, they were intelligent beings who knew exactly what they were doing.

They were systematically trying to wipe out humans.

Suddenly, the black Xathi dashed forward. Everyone scrambled to the back of the room, desperate to escape its grasp. But the Xathi already had its target planned out. It took hold of Anton, who screamed and thrashed in its grip.

Myself, Vidia, and a few others moved forward to help him.

Anton's pleading cry echoed through the room even after the metal door slammed shut again. But what I did not expect was for the two Xathi to appear in the next room over, the one we could see through the panels.

They dragged a still struggling Anton into the center of the room and strapped him to a table. He thrashed frantically, even when one of the Xathi pushed a long, thick needle into his ear.

I gently pushed Calixta's head down so she couldn't see anything, but I couldn't look away.

The room was a lab. The Xathi were experimenting on us. When they removed the probe, they plugged it into one of the foreign machines, which immediately flickered to life.

I didn't understand what they were measuring or the reading they were getting but they didn't look pleased.

They scuttled back to Anton. Each Xathi took up one of his arms and one of his legs. In a movement so swift I could only process it after it had happened, they ripped him apart. The survivors screamed, moving as far away from the windows as they could.

"Gather the children and get them as far away from the door as possible," I heard Vidia command. I couldn't move. I watched in horror as one of the Xathi ate one of Anton's arms.

Someone took Calixta from me. Her cries sounded far away, like a fading echo. I couldn't look away from the pile of blood and bones that had once been a person.

I felt myself closing off from the other people around me. I needed to think. I needed to examine the facts. I could figure this out if I just had a moment to think.

The door snapped open again and the Xathi came through to collect their next victim. They chose another man, larger and sturdier than Anton was, but he was still no match for them.

A woman ran forward but the others restrained her. She fought against them, screaming and sobbing.

"I love you, Miguel!" she cried.

I could practically feel her heart as it cracked open.

"I love you, Leticia," the man, Miguel, yelled back before the door closed again.

Vidia immediately went to console Leticia, who had crumpled to the ground.

I watched, unblinking, as the Xathi strapped Miguel to the same table that was still covered in Anton's blood. They performed the same test and measured the results in the same way.

But Miguel wasn't ripped to shreds. Instead, they injected him with something that appeared to render him unconscious and ushered him into another room.

Data. This was data. Something I could work with. Something I could measure.

I began to pace frantically. There were pieces of this puzzle scattered in front of me. I just had to put them together. I could do this.

One result means food, I thought. That was pretty obvious. The other result means…a successful injection of something. Something like the language implants Jeneva and the others had back on the ship? Maybe. A successful injection of…something without side effects? Okay. It wasn't much but it was a starting place.

What were the Xathi after? They were an advanced species physically and technologically. What were they missing?

My thoughts chased themselves in the same circles over and over until pain sprung up between my temples. I continued to pace even as the Xathi came and took more people for their tests.

I paced through screaming children and crying loved ones. I could solve this problem. I could fix all of this if I could just think.

I walked to the darkest corner of the room, as far away from the others as I could manage. I sat with my back pressed against the icy metal and squeezed my eyes shut.

The ones the Xathi don't like get eaten. All I have to do is figure out which people those are and make sure they get taken last.

Wait, no. That isn't right. Too much conjecture. Not

enough facts. Not enough data. No data. No data. No data.

I didn't realize I was crying until I choked on a sob. I couldn't solve this problem. People were dying and they were going to keep dying. There was nothing I could do about it.

There was no magic equation to make it all better. There was no process to follow to get the results I wanted.

It was just me and the cold and the darkness.

"Axtin," I moaned quietly. I needed him. I wanted him to wrap me in his strong arms and tell me that everything was going to be okay.

I would do anything to see him again. I would give up my life's research if it meant I could see him again, if it meant an end to the slaughter.

"Axtin, please save me," I whispered into the darkness. The darkness didn't answer.

AXTIN

It only took us two hours to make it to the Xathi ship, but that was two hours that the Xathi had Leena and the others. Two hours for them to have done whatever it is that they do to their prisoners. I needed to get in there.

But Vrehx held me back. "Look at the ship, do you see any openings?"

I took a look.

The thing made the *Vengeance* look small, and we were one of the bigger ships in the fleet. A bit awkward, I couldn't figure out how the thing maneuvered when in flight; the Xathi ship was—when not broken— essentially two pyramids on top of one another.

When we were pulled through the rift, the top half of their ziggurat had broken off, leaving the bottom half—still a pretty big portion—to fall through and crash onto the planet.

The crash destroyed roughly half of Nyheim. Even now, weeks after our arrival, there was still some smoke rising into the air from parts of the city. From what the females told us, Nyheim had been the cultural, social, and economic center of the planet.

Now there was a massive gash in the ground for several miles, ending in the center of the city, the entire east and south sides obliterated. The rest of the city was in ruins.

The Xathi had been thorough in their search. It was unlikely any humans survived at all.

As for the ship itself, there were several points of entry, but each of those were guarded by at least a dozen Xathi soldiers, their blue shells vibrant against the gray of the ship. The black-shelled hunters roamed the city and walked patrol around the ship. Even some of the green-shelled farm-bugs worked some of the land just outside the crash site.

Too many Xathi to go in headfirst.

"Okay, you're right. We need to be smart about this. But we can't take too long, or they'll have already killed everyone."

"If they haven't been extinguished already," Takar remarked.

I snarled at him and he quickly held up a hand in apology.

"Easy, boys. Put the fangs away," Karzin cut in. He stared both of us down until we looked away. "Vrehx, this is your boy, your mission. Thoughts?"

Vrehx stayed quiet for several minutes. We knew he was thinking things through, but why did it have to take so long?

I was just about to lose my mind when he spoke.

"Okay. The current openings are no good to us, too heavily guarded. So, we need to make our own door."

I perked up a bit. I did enjoy watching things go boom.

"Our only problem once we're inside is that we don't know where the humans are being held. Too big an area to search within a reasonable time."

"I can help with that," Tu'ver said.

We all looked at him in anticipation.

"I will use my disguise holo and get captured. When they take me to the others, I will broadcast our position. Then you come and rescue us all."

He was insanely calm, and that unnerved me to no end. He was willing to let himself be captured, and he'd have to do it unarmed, and he was as calm as he would be choosing his morning meal.

"That might work," Karzin admitted. "And while he's

in there, we'll set some charges around the ship to make our way in."

"I'll get the charges," I said, but Vrehx held up a finger and tilted his head.

"I've got a better idea. Tu'ver, do what you need, leave your weapons with us. Only take what you're confident you can hide on your person without being detected. We're going to need a distraction to let whoever is setting the charges have time to set them." He looked at me and smiled. "You want to be a distraction?"

I smiled back. "Oh, yeah. You know I do."

"Then we're the distraction. You want in on this, Karzin?"

The older Valorni shook his head. "As much as I would love to kill some bugs, I've got a slightly better idea. The brothers love to fight, as does Sylor. Take those three to create your distraction. The rest of us will set the charges and come back around to bail your asses out when things get too out of hand."

With a smile on his face, Vrehx nodded. "That will do. How long to set the charges?"

"We won't go around the whole ship. It's too big, too much debris, too many hunters. We'll concentrate on this side we can see, so…two minutes?"

"Do it. Sakev, Dax, make sure his back doesn't get torn up and those charges don't end up in Xathi control." The two nodded and left with Karzin. Rokul, Takar, and Sylor came over, each of them serious.

"Thoughts?" It took a second to realize Vrehx was asking me.

"You know me...I've always loved a head-on collision."

"That you have. Fine, let's get over there," he said, pointing off to our right where the trees thinned out. "We'll come out over there and try to draw as many of the Xathi over as we can. No one dies, that's an order."

"Sir!" was the universal response.

We headed over towards where Vrehx had pointed.

"Listen, Axtin," Vrehx said to me, drawing me to one side. "I apologize for having doubted you and your feelings. No, I'm not the only one 'allowed' to have a human and I was wrong to make you feel that way. You're right, if this was Jeneva, I would have been the first to rush in."

"Apology accepted," I said with a toothy grin. "To borrow a phrase from Jeneva, she certainly took that stick out of your ass."

"What?"

"She's been good for you. It means that you're not as rigid as you used to be. It's almost like you're one of us now."

"She has been good for me, and you deserve the same. I'm sorry to have made you feel otherwise."

"And I apologize for pushing you around and yelling at you. It was wrong to make you feel like a weakling," I said, as the old camaraderie of warriors returned.

He was about to say something when he saw me turn away, hiding a smile. "Ass."

I stifled a laugh, wouldn't do to announce our position to the Xathi yet. Then our earpieces crackled as Tu'ver's voice came on. He was being captured, broadcasting it to us.

"Easy, yeh frakin' buggahs." He was imitating some of the native slang. "I said 'easy.' No need fo pushin'." Several seconds passed before we heard him again. His voice was low, like he was whispering. "Infiltration complete. In elevator. Up."

Another few seconds passed. "Five levels. Now is good."

"You heard him, time for a distraction." I stood up, walked out of the trees, and howled at the Xathi.

As the others came out behind me, the Xathi perked up, chittered amongst themselves, and then approached. Of the nearly three dozen soldiers and hunters roaming outside, only seven remained behind.

"Five against twenty-six. Five apiece with one to spare. It has been a good fight, friends," Rokul said as he brought his rifle to his shoulder.

"That it has, my brother. May we extinguish as many of our enemies as we can," Takar added.

"Oh, just shut up and kill the srell."

I guess Sylor was tired of the brothers being philosophical all the time. I nodded at Sylor, took out a grenade, flipped the pin, and threw. Sylor howled as he took aim, shooting the grenade before it hit the ground.

The explosion blew apart three Xathi and sent several others flying. Sylor and I let out twin howls and charged, both of us shooting on the run. Vrehx and the brothers were a few paces behind, providing controlled fire.

I found myself laughing as I put away my blaster and reached back for my hammer. The two berserkers were leading the charge. It was going to be fun fighting side-by-side with Sylor.

We crashed into the Xathi with force, my hammer clearing a path as it left Xathi arms, legs, and chunks lying on the ground. Sylor was to my right, jumping and flipping around, his blasters firing away. Vrehx let out a howl as he slid under a hunter, his knife extended upward, slicing through the underbelly.

I could see the brothers methodically firing away with their rifles, shooting anything that tried to get behind us.

A hunter managed to slice my arm, but I barely noticed as I kicked it in the chest. It fell against a soldier, impaling itself on the soldier's mandible. As it tried to shake the hunter off, I swung once. As the

Xathi's ribcage shattered under my hammer, blood spewed from its mouth.

Sylor screamed.

I turned to see him surrounded, his blasters flipped in his hands. He was using them as makeshift hammers. Vrehx was fighting two on his own, the brothers were firing away, so it was up to me.

I yelled an ancient Valorni battle cry and rushed in. I arrived as one of the soldiers bit down on Sylor's leg, making him howl in pain. I hurtled into the fray, kicking one in the head as I flew over. My hammer clipped the one that bit Sylor and ricocheted out of my hands.

It was enough to get the Xathi to let go, and I quickly grabbed its head and twisted, its neck snapping loudly.

I grabbed my blasters and stood over Sylor, firing away at the Xathi. He grabbed a grenade from my hip pack and tossed it just outside the circle. We threw ourselves to the ground just as the "thwump" of the grenade blew a hole in the ground. I got back to my feet and fired at the Xathi that were disoriented.

I took a quick look around. Of the twenty-six that first attacked us, half were dead or injured, but Vrehx was engaged in hand-to-hand, the brothers were now forced into close-quarters combat, and Sylor and I still had five or six surrounding us.

I was breathing hard, Sylor was bleeding and barely able to stand, and my hammer was too far away.

Our distraction might prove to be my last charge.

I clicked on the comm to Tu'ver. "Thank you, my friend, for helping me try to save Leena. Just get her out safely is all I ask."

I clicked the comm off and reloaded.

The Xathi took two steps towards us, then the explosions roared through the air, turning their attention away from us. Karzin and the others had finally done their part. Sylor, bum leg and all, and I didn't waste the opportunity.

We attacked.

The others came rushing over, controlling their fire to make sure they didn't hit us. It was close, though. Just as I was about to kick one, its head exploded from a rifle shot.

I looked up and Dax saluted me before taking aim and firing again.

The seven bugs that had stayed behind to guard the entrances had joined the fight, but three grenades blew them to pieces. I could hear the brothers laughing.

The nine of us took down the remaining Xathi. Vrehx took care of Sylor's leg with some med-foam and a wrap, the rest of us reloaded our weapons.

I got my hammer back.

A silent moment passed between us as we looked at

one another. The Xathi knew we were here, and they wouldn't let us in quietly.

I looked at all of them, then turned and headed towards the ship.

I wasn't leaving without Leena.

LEENA

I had to remind myself to breathe, to force the air into my lungs through sheer force of will. It hurt. Just existing seemed to hurt now.

I would love to say that I found some inner strength in those moments—a small kernel of bravery that propelled me back into reality—but that would be a lie. In truth, I probably would've laid there forever, trembling on the cold floor as people continued to be slaughtered around me.

It was only the thought of Calixta that pulled me back from the brink. Nothing but the small girl at my side could've moved me then.

"Leena?" Her voice shook as she spoke, heavy with the kind of overwhelming fear that I was just coming to know.

I sat up with a groan, the world swaying as I did so. My eyes felt raw from tears, my hands still shaking from the force of my breakdown.

"Calixta," I croaked. "Are you okay?"

Tears cut tracks down her grime-coveredcheeks, her eyes still wide with shock, but she nodded, nonetheless.

I opened my arms, gesturing for her to come nearer. With a whimper, she climbed into my lap, burying her face into me as if she could shut out the world.

I wished she could. I wished, more than anything, that I could offer this sweet girl some level of true safety. But we both knew it was beyond me. It was beyond us both now.

The Xathi were worse than I had understood, stronger, more vicious. In my world before they arrived, I could never have even imagined beings that possessed such a level of cold indifference to life.

I looked across at them, watching as they continued to process the humans at an alarming rate. There were no feelings in their actions—no hint of a consciousness beyond hunger. It was terrifying to witness, even more so knowing that it was only a matter of time before they turned their attention to us.

About a third of the humans had been processed, the fraction remaining looking on in various stages of defeat. It broke my heart to see it. These people were survivors, the last of their town.

For the briefest of moments, they must've imagined that they had made it, that they were coming out the other side.

And now this.

I couldn't bear to look. I lay my head back against the wall, closing my eyes as I pulled Calixta tighter against me.

This was the end. After all the fighting, all the pointless resistance, this was how our story came to a close—huddled on the floor, clinging to each other like life rafts.

I thought of Mariella then, feeling tears sting my eyes. I should've said goodbye when I had the chance. But of course, I didn't.

I was too stubborn, too sure. I had told myself that saying goodbye was the same as admitting the risk—that if I saved it for later, there would have to be a later.

It was childish. Stupid. And it had cost me a moment that I would never get back.

I could've stewed in that misery forever, or at least until the Xathi came for me, but I was drawn from my thoughts, the sound of approaching footsteps forcing my eyes to open.

As my blurred vision focused, I looked up at the newcomer, a large man I didn't recognize. I instinctively redoubled my grip on Calixta, startling her as I flinched backward, away as the Xathi shoved him into the cell.

"Leena," the man said, crouching down to our level. "Don't be afraid. It's me, Tu'ver." He gestured in the general direction of his belt, drawing my eyes to the cloaking device attached to it.

My heart leapt in my chest.

"Tu'ver?" I sat up in a rush, leaning in to speak discreetly. "Where's Axtin?"

"Don't worry. He and the rest of the crew are on their way in. We're going to get you out of here."

I opened my mouth to reply, but there were no words for the gratitude I felt in that moment. I stuttered, trying and failing to stop the tears of joy that sprang to my eyes. It was no use.

Axtin was coming for me. I had never in my life heard sweeter words.

I reached for Tu'ver's hand, clinging to him as I sobbed openly. In my lap, Calixta had sat up, tentative hope flashing in her eyes.

"Really?" she asked.

Tu'ver seemed to notice her for the first time. A smile touched his lips as he nodded.

"Really."

She turned to me, throwing her arms around me in a fierce hug. It was like coming back to life.

"Thank you so much," I said, tears still streaming from my eyes. "I can't believe you're here. You're risking your life!"

"Well, Mariella asked me. Begged, really. I promised I'd do whatever I could to get you out."

Mariella.

It was all I could do not to start sobbing all over again.

"But how did you find us?" I asked, turning back to Tu'ver. "How did you even get in here?"

How he could go from unassuming hero to completely smug so quickly is beyond me, but somehow he managed it.

He cocked his head to the side. "Stealth and sneak attacks are my specialty. I would've thought you'd been informed."

I never thought I'd laugh again, but I found myself doing it anyway, giggling into the top of Calixta's dark hair while she looked at me as if I'd gone insane. To be fair, I probably had. At least a little bit.

My mirth didn't last, though. Of course it didn't. For a moment, with Tu'ver there, it was easy to forget how dire our circumstances were.

The Xathi, though, were quick to remind me.

It was the sound again—the one that had notified me of their presence to begin with. Nonstop, an ever-present background noise since we arrived in this awful place, but now it drew nearer.

I looked past Tu'ver at the one that was approaching from behind him. It, like all the others, wore an expression of cold indifference. If you could even call it an expression, that is.

I wasn't sure if the Xathi were even capable of making more than one face.

It was probably best that they didn't, though; the one they had was already gruesome enough. I stared into it as the creature approached, its mouth opening to reveal rows of jutting teeth.

This planet was full of monsters, a fact I'd recently been reminded of since journeying into the forest. None of the others, though, came anywhere near the level of sheer horror that the Xathi existed on.

They were nightmare made reality, death incarnate. And now one headed straight for us.

I pulled Calixta tighter against me, gripping her in what I'm sure was a painful embrace, just as the beast reached us. I wasn't about to let go, especially not as the monster's eyes fell to her.

The Xathi ignored Tu'ver entirely; it ignored me. Its sole focus was the small child in my arms. It leaned forward, insectile arms snaking out toward her.

She screamed, sheer terror rocking her tiny body as she pushed tighter against me.

I dug my feet into the floor, desperately shoving us backward even as the wall bit painfully into my shoulders. There was nowhere to go, nowhere to run, but my body refused to accept it.

All I knew was that I wouldn't let this beast have Calixta, no matter what it took.

Tu'ver stood between us and the door to the cage, but the Xathi knocked him aside with a hard blow. Terror wrapped my vision until all I could see was the Xathi soldier. All I could hear were Calixta's screams.

It grabbed at her, its clawed limbs scraping against her delicate skin in a desperate attempt to rip her from my arms. I could already see the scratches forming, see small lines of blood appearing on her bare arms.

I kicked madly at it, my feet landing completely unnoticed against the crystalline exoskeleton. It merely snarled, not relenting in its task.

"Over here, ugly!" Tu'ver shouted as he rolled to his feet. From his waist he unwound a trail of silver; with a snap of his wrist, it turned into a lethal-looking long baton. Dancing between us and the Xathi, he kept shouting until I had Calixta safe in the back corner.

The creature turned toward the newly realized threat, its body puffing in challenge. I knew that Tu'ver could kill it; I didn't doubt it for a second. But my heart raced in my chest nonetheless.

The Xathi were a hive mind. What would happen if

Tu'ver did manage to take this one out? How long before the rest of them swarmed?

I pushed myself to my feet, still clutching Calixta in a death grip as my eyes scanned the room before us.

None of the others seemed to have noticed us yet. Either that, or they were unconcerned about what they perceived to be a scuffle with a couple of humans.

How long before that changed?

I turned to Tu'ver, watching as he cocked back his arm, preparing to deliver a truly devastating blow. My mouth opened to object, a million thoughts pouring through my mind.

We couldn't kill the thing, not without bringing the entire horde down on our heads. Master of stealth or not, even Tu'ver couldn't save us from that.

I wanted to tell him to stop, that fighting wouldn't save us this time. We had to run, and we had to go now.

"Tu'ver!" I shouted. "We hav—"

I never got to finish my sentence.

A bone-rattling blast cut through the noise, the walls of the room shaking from the intensity.

All movement stopped. Every head, Xathi and human, turned in the direction of the sound.

For a moment that seemed much longer, we stayed that way. The processing had halted, the horrors paused.

Then, as one, the Xathi began to move.

Tu'ver's weapon hung forgotten in the air as the soldier before us turned, heading toward the source of the blast.

They fell immediately into formation, every creature in the room surging toward the exits as the rest of us watched on in wonder.

In no time at all, the last of them had funneled through the doorway, silence reigning in their wake.

I looked at Tu'ver, my mouth hanging open in surprise.

He deactivated his disguise and smiled. "That's our cue."

AXTIN

I was the first one in the ship and the first one to shoot. Two Xathi down before I was three steps into their ship. The others were a few paces behind.

Based on the location Tu'ver gave us, it would take us several minutes to get there on a clean run. Knowing the Xathi would be in the way, we'd have to take it slow and smart, and that meant more time—more time for the Xathi to harm the humans, more time for them to harm Leena, more time for her to die.

No. No. That wasn't going to happen.

My breath was coming fast. I was nearly hyperventilating.

I had to hurry. I had to hurt the Xathi. I had to get to Leena.

I was in a hallway, Tu'ver's beacon pulling me

forward. I wanted my hammer, I wanted Leena, but the hall was too small for my hammer to be used effectively, and Leena was five levels above me.

A hunter came out of an aperture to my left. I punched it in the face, grabbed it, turned it around, and shot it in its sweet spot on the back of the neck, killing it quickly. I tossed a grenade down the aperture and walked away, the explosion behind me barely making me stumble.

I could hear Vrehx and Karzin yelling out orders and calling out to me, but I kept going. I *was* going slow, at least by my standards.

I *was* being careful. There were more dead Xathi than wounds on me, so that meant careful.

"Axtin!"

I ignored Vrehx and kept going. Two more Xathi came down the passageway; I opened fire on both. One dropped quickly, the other ducked back into another passageway.

They were getting smarter. They weren't relying on brute force and numbers anymore.

I continued and came up to the intersection within a few seconds. I peeked around the corner and nearly lost my head as one of the Xathi's claws brushed against my scalp.

I felt a sticky wetness down the back of my head and neck and cursed myself for being stupid. I ducked down low and brought my blaster around, firing away. The clip emptied as the Xathi fell on me.

I couldn't breathe. I had no leverage; my arm was pinned awkwardly. I tried to push, but I got no movement.

Tilting my head up to look down the hall, I could see two hunters coming my way. Then the brothers stepped into view, firing at the hunters and killing them. Dax and Sakev pulled the Xathi off me, and Vrehx pulled me to my feet.

"You done acting like an impulsive fool?"

With a shrug, I said, "Probably not."

He rolled his eyes and grinned. "At least you're being honest with me. No more rushing ahead. You're no good to Leena dead, got that?"

I nodded. He was right. If I was dead, Leena would be alone, and I wasn't going to leave her alone.

I cared about her too much to leave her alone. "Fine, but we can't go slow. The slower we go, the more chance she and Tu'ver die."

"Agreed," he said. "But we can't be careless, either. Understand?"

"Understood," I said with sincerity.

"Good. Brothers, lead the way. Dax, Sakev, bring up the rear. Axtin, reload and let's go."

I reloaded my blasters as we went ahead.

It was time to go save my beloved.

One by one, the Xathi left to investigate the noise. Though I had every reason to believe it was Axtin and the others here to rescue us, I couldn't make myself hope that I'd see him again.

"Do you know where they are?" I asked Tu'ver.

"I could see them on my nav unit right up until they boarded the ship." He shrugged.

"How come you were able to send a signal and I wasn't?" Vidia asked, looking at her own completely unresponsive nav unit.

"These markings aren't just decoration," Tu'ver said, gesturing to the intricate pattern of circuits fused into his skin suit. "My augmentations are more resistant to whatever the Xathi are using to scramble our tech. This," he tapped at the baton, "takes its charge from my own bio-electricity. Not as powerful as a full-sized blaster, but it gets the job done."

"I see," Vidia said, peering closer at Tu'ver's implants. "When we survive this, you'll have to tell me more. It's fascinating."

"Gladly." Tu'ver nodded.

Vidia turned to me. "Let's work on getting everyone organized so we can make a run for it," she said.

"What?" I blurted. The idea was absurd, and no one here was in any sort of shape to run through a Xathi ship. "Axtin and the others know where we are. If we move, we could lose them completely."

"It's too risky to assume they'll live long enough to make it to this room," Vidia argued. "Besides, your friend here said their nav points aren't going to work inside the ship. They have an idea where we are, at best."

The thought of Axtin never making it to us, the thought of him dying horribly somewhere on this ship while trying to rescue me, was unbearable.

"Okay." I nodded. I wasn't comfortable with this plan by any means, but it looked like it was the best option in a terrible situation.

"I'll go check the nearby corridors to make sure there are no surprises," Tu'ver volunteered.

"Everyone!" Vidia shouted.

The survivors' heads snapped to attention. There

were so few of us now. Our numbers were less than half of what they were when we were herded into this torture chamber.

"We're going to make a run for it. Grab anything that can be used as a weapon. Arm yourselves. If we're going down, we're going down fighting. I refuse to die like an animal in a holding pen!"

Her brief speech inspired the weary survivors. Immediately, they set to work, picking apart the sparse room for anything that could be used for defense.

Very little came to hand.

Tu'ver eased out the doorway, then waved for us to follow. I picked up Calixta, careful of her cuts. "We're going to try to get out of here, but I need you to be quiet, okay?"

She wrapped her thin arms around my neck and clung tightly, silently nodding her agreement.

"Good girl," I said, giving her a squeeze.

"Leena!" Vidia called my name, waiting by the doorway with a group of survivors. " I want you and Tu'ver at the front. You're going to lead us through the ship."

"What?" I sputtered.

"The two of you know more about Xathi ships than we do," Vidia reasoned.

"Not by much!" I exclaimed.

"It's our best option," Vidia said with a shrug. "I'm

going to be the last one out. I'll cover our tail and help anyone who's falling behind."

She quickly moved through the crowd, repeating her plan to each of the survivors and telling them where they should be in the group.

"Any advice?" I asked Tu'ver. I appreciated his steady mannerism, especially since I felt so frayed. I was glad he had been there for Mariella.

"The far wall of this room is curved, suggesting that we are against the hull," Tu'ver said thoughtfully. "However, Xathi ships don't follow any sort of traditional ship blueprint, so I can't say for certain."

"So we're flying blind," I surmised.

"Essentially." Tu'ver nodded. "Based on the construction of more traditional ships, I would suggest going to the right."

"Right it is then." I sighed.

I gave a silent signal to those who had fallen in behind us. Vidia had divided the stronger, healthier survivors into two groups, one in the front with us, the rest guarding the rear with her. The injured held each other up, limping in the middle.

No one spoke as we dashed through the labyrinth of corridors. I turned without thinking. If I thought about which way to go too much, I would end up frozen with indecision.

These people, for whatever reason, believed I was

their best chance of getting out of here alive. I just had to keep hoping I would run into Axtin and the others. He would be waiting for me around the next turn, or the one after that.

He was here somewhere. I would find him. Or he would find me.

I realized I was mouthing his name with every step I took. We reached another divide. I dove left, so sure that Axtin was going to be around the bend.

But we were wrong.

At the end of the hallway, shrieking and thrashing with rage as they scuttled toward us, was a Xathi sub-queen and her soldiers, energy whips crackling in the air. Beside me, Tu'ver drew his blaster, ready to fight. Those who were behind us lifted their weapons, but I could sense the hesitation in their bodies.

In front of a swarm of massive crystalized bug creatures, a handful of weakened humans with a few makeshift weapons looked like children in a play fight.

The Xathi sub-queen drew up to her full height. She appeared to be intently focused on me. In a way I couldn't possibly explain, I felt the sheer spite in her gaze.

She knew I was the one who helped Vidia and the others escape. One of the Xathi Axtin killed must've seen me before it died.

My mind spun, cycling and circling, assembling data and options until only one thing stood clear.

"Take her!" I shoved Calixta into Tu'ver's arms and grabbed for his weapon. "Get the others out of here."

"This is insane!" Tu'ver protested as Calixta wriggled against him, trying to get back to me. "I'm not leaving you here."

"You have to," I said, my voice surprisingly level. "You have to tell Mariella what happened. You need to be there for her." *When I no longer am,* I added silently. Tu'ver opened his mouth to protest again, but I cut him off.

"The more you stand there and argue, the more likely you won't leave this ship at all," I said desperately. "You can't tell me you don't have more surprises hidden in all of that," I waved at his circuitry. "They need you more than me."

But it was too late. The Xathi sub-queen and her soldiers were upon us.

I fired Tu'ver's weapon wildly, striking one of the soldiers in the leg. Its crystalized exoskeleton chipped and cracked a little bit, but I didn't do any real damage.

The sub-queen reared up and used her front legs to shove me to the ground. My head collided with the metal floor hard enough to make me see stars.

I could barely see anything, there was a deafening

ringing in my ears. I could only hope that Tu'ver had taken the chance to run.

I did my best, I thought as the spear-like tip of the sub-queen's leg pieced my arm. I closed my eyes. I didn't want the last thing I saw to be her face.

I thought of Mariella, Calixta, and Axtin. Maybe my death would bring them together into a strange but good surrogate family. Yeah, that would be good for Calixta.

I believed she would like Mariella. Mariella was always good with children. She'd probably be afraid of Axtin at first, but as soon as she saw his gentle side, I think she'd adore him.

They would be okay.

I released a final breath. I was at peace with this.

Above me, I heard a terrible crack, loud enough to cancel out the ringing in my ears. I opened my eyes. The sub-queen's head was split down the middle by a perfectly aimed blaster shot.

AXTIN

The beacon kept moving.

"Srell. Where the blazes is Tu'ver taking them?"

"He might not have had a choice, Vrehx. We need to split up," Karzin suggested.

"No," Vrehx commanded. "If we run into a horde of soldiers, we'll need all the firepower."

"You make a good point," he acquiesced. "Which direction then?"

We were standing at an intersection about thirty yards from where we came up. This floor was much more manufactured than the ones below, looking very much like an actual starship than a cave system like the first floor.

Behind us was the elevator. Then to our left, right,

and in front were three passageways that all looked the same. The only thing that gave us any kind of hint on where to go was the beacon, which was moving more on the right than on the left.

"Look, the beacon's somewhere in that direction," I said as I pointed roughly between the right and forward hall. "Let's just pick one and go. The longer we sit here, the worse things get."

"But which passageway?" Vrehx asked aloud.

He had a point. Which one? If we picked the wrong one, it would waste so much time that we couldn't afford.

But if we sat here thinking about it all day, that would be just as bad of a waste. My mind started imagining what they were doing to Leena, or had already done to Leena, and my heart was pounding so hard it started to hurt.

My breathing was hard, my head hurt, my wounds hurt, my wrist was killing me, and all of it made me want to save her even more.

I looked at the beacon. I tried to do a quick calculation in my head, then I took off down the front corridor. I didn't bother waiting for the others; I just went.

There was just something in my mind, screaming at me to hurry. The others called after me and started to follow, but for some reason, they weren't able to catch up to me.

Every intersection that I came across, I just somehow knew which direction to take. Something was pulling me. It kept telling me where to go, and I just went.

I heard gunfire and yelling behind me. I looked back and saw the others fighting some Xathi. I knew I should turn back to help, but the pull had become impossible to resist.

I couldn't turn back. I had to keep moving on.

A green Xathi, a farmer, jumped out at me, chittering at what seemed like a million miles an hour. Then it snapped at me, pushing me back. I pulled out my blaster and shot it.

It fell like a rock, its armor not nearly as thick as a hunter's or soldier's. Another farmer jumped out at me, trying to grab me. I shot it, too.

Six more farmers attacked, six more farmers dropped. Without the suits to augment their strength, they were no match for us.

The Xathi that came out of the corridors behind me were cut down quickly by the others. More workers and farmers, their shells much thinner than those of the soldiers. The farmers dropped easily, the workers nearly so.

It should've been a concern in my mind. It should've been something that worried me, but I kept going.

I was still being pulled, and my only hope was that it was toward Leena. The beacon *was* getting closer, so I didn't doubt the sensation.

The corridors twisted and turned, until whatever pulled me to Leena thrummed in my head.

Finally, there were screams.

Human screams.

A sub-queen reared above Leena, deflecting the steady stream of shots Tu'ver fired into her iridescent carapace.

The pull vanished, replaced by rage.

My blaster wasn't one of Tu'ver's easily hideable toys. Charging through the crowd of humans scrambling past us in the corridor, I fired.

And the the sub-queen's head split down the middle.

The Xathi soldiers went into a frenzy.

And the room erupted in chaos and blood.

LEENA

I sat on a fallen tree long since hollowed out and gently traced my fingers over the moss that covered it. The bioluminescent plant seemed to react to my presence. It glowed brighter at my touch.

All around me, the forest was alight. Plants glowed in the falling dusk. Dim light still fought its way through the canopy overhead, but even as I watched, it started to fade.

Part of me recognized this place. A small voice insisted that I crawl into the log and hide from the creatures that lived in the darkness. But I knew, deep in my heart, that it was wrong.

Because this wasn't Ankau. This wasn't a planet crawling with monsters.

There were no carnivorous vines here and no

gigantic spiders. Those things were bedtime stories—myths designed to keep children from going too far astray.

This forest had no monsters. This *planet* had no monsters. I was safe here and always had been.

"I told you it was beautiful."

I turned to the voice, smiling as Axtin stepped into view.

"You're right," I said. "It was worth the trip."

He sat beside me, stilling my hand as he took it in one of his.

"What was that?" he asked, smiling mischievously, "Srell, Leena, are you saying I was... *right?*"

I laughed, swatting playfully at his shoulder. "Okay, okay, don't get used to it."

"Oh, believe me, I won't."

The comment earned him another swat, but I smiled even wider. "You shouldn't let them go too far." I turned back to the forest.

"Ah, you worry too much. They're just having fun."

"Still..."

"They know not to wander, Leena. Besides, this gives us a minute alone. When was the last time we had that?"

I tapped my chin, looking up to the side in dramatic thought.

"Hmm, that would be... well, never," I said teasingly.

He chuckled, pulling me closer to plant a kiss on my neck. Even that had sparks flooding through me. Even after all this time, I was nothing but putty in his hands.

"You see my point then?" he asked, nuzzling against me with a groan.

"I'm starting to."

Just then, the sound of laughter reached my ears, quickly followed by the rustling of leaves.

"Momma!"

I laughed, perfect timing as usual.

They tore into the clearing, both of them beaming in delight. Their clothes were mussed, and their faces were smudged with dirt.

"Guess what we found!" Zyta demanded, turning to smile at her giggling brother.

"What did you find?" Axtin asked, leaning over in genuine curiosity.

"Show them!" Zyta insisted, nudging her brother forward.

He crossed to us, palms cupped before him and a smile pulling at his lips.

"Look!" He opened his hands the barest inch, gazing down at his discovery in pure wonder. "It's a firebug!"

I leaned in to look, noting the blue glow emitting from his hands.

Sure enough, there it was. The little creature crawled frantically along his palms, its light shining brighter than I would have thought possible, like a small ember in a forest of living flame.

"It's amazing," I said, genuinely meaning it.

"I know," Zyta said, "and there's more! They're all over the place!"

Axtin turned to me, looking every bit as excited as the children. "Care to go for a walk?"

I nodded. "Show us the way."

We stood, watching as the children turned in the general direction from which they'd come.

"It's this way!"

I followed, my feet sinking into the densely carpeted ground.

We'd only gone a few steps when I heard the rustling. I stopped mid-stride, gazing around in question.

"Wait, did you hear that?"

"Hear what?" Axtin asked, coming to a stop along with the kids.

"I think there's something out here."

"It's probably a rabbit."

I shook my head, feeling chills that I couldn't explain break over my skin. "No, no I don't think so."

Axtin laughed, walking back over to me. "Sweetie, there's nothing out here. No monsters, okay?"

He looked at me patiently, offering his hand.

Of course, there was nothing out here. This was a safe place.

I opened my mouth to apologize when I heard it again, closer this time. Very close.

"Axtin…"

But it was too late.

She tore into the clearing. Her crystalline legs churned up the untouched earth as she charged toward us.

My mouth fell open in shock, and my feet seemed to glue themselves to the ground.

A Xathi sub-queen. And she was going to kill us all.

"Run, kids!" Axtin screamed, turning toward her.

A hammer had somehow materialized in his hands. The shape of it was achingly familiar, though I'd never seen it before.

I turned to the children and watched as they disappeared into the trees. I could hear their screams as they ran, their sheer terror making my heart skip a beat.

"Run, Leena!" Axtin shouted.

But I couldn't. My legs were cemented to the earth, and my voice was lost in the horror of the creature before us. I was paralyzed.

The Xathi queen turned to me, and her eyes seemed to bore into my mind. I wanted to run, to fight, to do anything… but all I could do was watch as she ran toward me.

"I said *run*, Leena!"

She was so close now. It was almost over.

I knew it, deep in my core. This was how it ended.

The thought brought a strange sense of déjà vu—a memory, buried deep.

I'd never know where it came from, though. There was no time to figure it out. She was almost upon me.

"Leena!"

Axtin came into view, hurling himself before me just as she arrived. His body shook with rage, that odd hammer still clenched in his fists.

"No!" he yelled, swinging his weapon with every ounce of his might.

I watched it as if in slow motion, a small flicker of hope sparking to life in my chest. Axtin could save me. He could save all of us.

His weapon descended in a perfect arc. The air around it seemed to ripple with the sheer force of his swing.

It landed with a small *clink*. It wasn't the sound of a hammer striking flesh, or crystal, or whatever that thing was made out of. It was like an ice cube dropped into a cup, so quiet as to barely be heard.

The beast roared, her fury loud enough to shake the earth.

"Axtin!" I screamed, finally finding my voice.

As always, it was far too late.

The monster reached down with her insectile arms, plucking the hammer from Axtin's hands as if she were taking a toy from a small child. She tossed it aside, her mouth twisting into a sick imitation of a smile.

I knew what was coming.

I tried to look away, but my eyes refused to close, and my head refused to turn.

I opened my mouth to scream, but the sound was lost as the sub-queen roared once more.

Then, with grotesque ease, she reached for Axtin. In a single, fluid motion, she had him in her grasp. His feet lifted from the ground, his legs kicking futilely as her claws began their ghastly work.

Blood rained down on the luminous plants, on the vines, and on me. Hot and slick, it poured down around us, drenching the forest floor.

Axtin didn't scream. He didn't even make a sound as she tore into him, spilling his life and blood in a seemingly endless stream.

I opened my mouth again, willing myself to scream, to move... to do absolutely anything.

This time, it worked.

I woke to the sound of my own horrified scream, jolting upright as the noise tore its way through me.

My head spun, my body swayed. I could feel my

heart pounding in my chest as my lungs struggled for air. All I could see was Axtin, his limp body clutched in the hands of the sub-queen.

I shook my head, trying to erase the image as I gazed around the room.

"Leena?"

I turned towards the sound, finding Mariella at my side.

"What? Where?"

"Leena, are you alright?" she asked, reaching for my hand.

I turned away, searching the room.

My eyes fell on him in the next moment, laying perfectly still in the bed beside mine.

Axtin.

My heart raced faster as I stared across his unconscious form. Bandages lined his body, his chest rising in small, uneven spurts.

The dream came rushing back to me—the horror. I could practically feel his blood and could hear my children's screams.

"Leena," Mariella repeated, squeezing my hand. "Talk to me."

I could hardly breath.

"I need to get out of here," I said, throwing one more look at Axtin. "Get me out of here."

"Leena, you need to stay and rest..." she began, but I didn't let her finish.

I didn't want to hear it. I didn't want to hear anything.

Axtin was hurt. The thought of him dying to save me made me feel ill and made my head swim all over again.

"No," I said, pulling the blankets quickly aside, "I have to go." I jumped from the bed, swaying only slightly before I steadied myself.

"You're confused," Mariella started, but I didn't stick around to hear more.

I reached for the door, almost running in my need to escape. I couldn't handle it—not any of it. So many people had died, and so many others were hurt.

I needed to get away from it. I didn't want to think about it or feel it.

I rushed into the hall, flying down the corridor in an outright panic. I just couldn't do it—not anymore.

The lab doors appeared, looking at me like a shining beacon. I threw myself at them, stumbling into the lab with a sigh.

This was where I belonged.

I would never leave again.

AXTIN

My dreams were confused blurs, snippets of stories that I was far too exhausted to follow.

The Xathi were there, making guest appearances in my thoughts like the overgrown pests they were. I was used to seeing them in my head—they'd obsessed me for years.

I paid them little mind.

Leena was there, too.

Flashes of her face, her smile—those dreams I paid attention to.

I clung to them like the last life raft in a bad storm.

I woke slowly, not sure if the glimpses of the med bay were real or just another part of the illusion. The bright lights and the crisp white walls appeared for the shortest second, and then it would be back to blackness.

After about the tenth time it happened, I started to understand what was really going on. From there on, I fought for consciousness, slowly drawing the brief moments out, longer and longer.

Conversations drifted past me as I struggled my way back to the surface, little pieces of the talk going on around me. Tu'ver was there, I was sure of it, and Mariella, too.

But not the voice I craved.

"Leena," I croaked.

I couldn't remember a time my throat had ever felt so raw. It was like I'd spent the last few days vacationing on a desert island with nothing but salt water to drink.

"Axtin," Tu'ver said. "Welcome back."

"Leena," I repeated, not caring about anything else.

"Mariella, he's awake," he called out to the female.

I groaned, clearly not going to get any information from the two of them. I tried to sit up, determined to find her myself.

The moment I tried, though, I was pulled back to the bed. It was only then that I noticed the pain in my wrists. I looked down, seeing the ties that looped around my ankles and arms.

"What the—"

"Relax, friend," Tu'ver offered, leaning over me. "You were grievously wounded. Don't go trying to leave just yet."

"Srell, Tu'ver, what is this? Let me out of these things!"

My heart beat faster, my fists clenched in their bonds. After everything I've been through, these idiots tied me to a bed in med bay? Had they absolutely lost their minds?

"Axtin…"

"I said, let me *out*, Tu'ver! Where is she?"

I could feel my anger rising with each passing second, fury starting to burn deep in my core. I needed to see Leena, to know that she was alright.

"Tu'ver," Mariella said, walking over to him.

She pressed her hand to his chest, leaning in to speak quietly. "I need to talk to Axtin. Can you give us a minute?"

He looked hesitant, glancing from me to her and back again.

Really, what did he have to be so protective about?

I was quite clearly tied to the recking bed. Not that I was any kind of threat when I wasn't. Not to Leena's sister anyway, no matter how angry I was.

"Very well," he finally said, "I'll just be outside."

Mariella stood silently, waiting for him to go. The moment the door closed behind him, she turned to me.

"Can you let me out of these things?" I asked, shaking my wrists for emphasis.

She shook her head. "Sorry, doctor's orders."

I had to remind myself that it would do no good to absolutely lose it on Leena's sister. I groaned, biting my lip to control myself.

"If you're going to leave me tied to the bed, can you at least give me some water?"

She flushed slightly, apparently feeling guilty that she hadn't thought of it herself. She headed over to a tray, grabbing a pitcher and cup.

After downing an entire glass, I felt a little better.

"Where is she?" I asked, this time in a voice I could actually recognize as my own. "Is she well?"

I remembered seeing her collapse, but after that, my mind was a blank. I didn't think she had been too badly injured, or I hadn't anyway. But this silent treatment was starting to make me nervous.

If something had happened to her...

"She's fine, Axtin."

I breathed a sigh of relief, letting my head fall back onto the pillow.

"Can you let me out so I can go see her now? Where is she?"

She shifted her feet, looking suddenly very uncomfortable.

"What I mean is, she's fine *physically.*" She crossed to

the chair near my bed, sitting with a sigh of her own. "Mentally, well, that's another story."

I lifted my head again. The concern that had only so recently left flooded my chest once more.

"What do you mean?" I asked.

"She locked herself in the lab the day she woke up, and she hasn't been out since. She *refuses* to come out."

My thoughts spun, and my heart started to race. "Have you tried to talk to her?"

"Of course I have. But she won't listen to me, or anyone else for that matter."

"Oh srell," I said, feeling guilt pour through me in waves. "This is all my fault."

Her brow furrowed. "How could this possibly be your fault?"

"I didn't get to her fast enough! She was trapped there with those blasted monsters! I know what she saw there, what they did to those people." I sank against the pillows. "I've seen it. I should have been there sooner. I never should have left her to begin with!"

She ran a hand through her hair, taking her time to think before answering.

"Axtin, listen to me. This is not your fault. You only left because you had to. What other choice did you have? Leena understands that, trust me. She doesn't blame you."

"If that were true, she'd be here, not hiding in the

lab. She blames me, and she's right to. I dishonored us both."

"Oh, enough," she snapped, scooting her chair closer with an awful screech. "What's happening right now, that's not about you. It's about Leena. She's overwhelmed. She's hiding. Believe me, as someone who has known her my entire life, this is what she does."

I rolled my eyes, a habit I probably picked up from Leena.

"Axtin, Leena is scared right now, okay? And I know you think you understand, but you don't."

"Well then, enlighten me!" I half yelled.

She stared me down evenly, not flinching at my outburst. For the first time, I truly saw the family resemblance. When Mariella looked at me like that, it was Leena I saw.

"Leena isn't hiding in that damn lab from the Xathi," she said, her tone hard. "She's in there hiding from her *feelings*. Being emotionally vulnerable terrifies her. It always does."

She paused in thought for a moment. When she continued, her voice had softened.

"Look, you were hurt really bad, Axtin. That's why you're tied up. It's not to punish you or piss you off. It's so that you don't jump out of bed first thing and ruin all the doctors' hard work."

"But—"

"No, just listen. Leena freaked out when she saw how badly you had been injured. That's why she hid. She isn't mad at you. She's completely terrified of loving you."

That last part had my attention.

"Are you sure?" I asked.

Now she smiled, a ghost of one, sure, but a smile nonetheless.

"Positive. She wouldn't be in the state she's in right now if she didn't really care about you," she replied.

"I really care about her, too, Mariella. I would do anything for her, *will* do anything for her."

She nodded, seeming to relax at my words.

"Okay, good. Because right now, she needs you to get well. You don't need to jump up and play hero, you need to rest," she told me.

"But—"

"Nope. No buts. You're in here for a reason. Just relax for a bit, okay?"

I didn't like it, not one little bit.

I glanced back down at my bonds, suppressing a growl. It didn't appear that I had much choice in the matter.

"Fine, but you'll talk to Leena for me. Tell her I'm awake," I said.

"I will."

I nodded in response, letting my head fall back to the pillow.

"Okay, then. Just tell her I'm well. Tell her I really want to see her," I added.

"I'll tell her."

There was nothing else I could do. I pulled again at my ties, confirming the idea. Yeah, I was pretty well strapped down.

Mariella left the med bay and this time I didn't bother to suppress my growl. It's not like anyone was around to hear it.

I didn't care about resting or getting well.

I just needed to see Leena.

LEENA

My eyes ached.

My eyelids scratched every time I tried to blink.

I couldn't break focus. I couldn't think about how my eyes hurt, or how my chest started to hurt when I forgot to breathe.

The only thing that mattered was the data and numbers on the monitors. Those little symbols were everything.

I had surrounded myself with six monitors. Three projected the perfected formula for the scent bombs, as well as the results of more detailed simulations I'd been able to come up with over the past few hours.

Or was it days?

The other three contained my research.

While the data compiled from my first set of queries, my mind started to drift.

No.

Frantically, I pulled up the rest of my data and cross-referenced it with the medical records of everyone I could get my digital fingers on, both human and alien.

Maybe I shouldn't be looking through those files, but nothing but the research mattered now.

Nothing.

Not a thing of value in anyone's records. Just another dead end.

I slumped back in my chair, pulling at my hair. Something, something I was missing.

For a flickering second, I thought of strong green arms to hold me, but I shoved the memory aside.

Never again.

What else to try, what else?

My stomach gurgled. I might have been hungry, but I didn't have time to eat. I had work to do—far, far too much work.

Just as soon as I could remember what the next simulation should be.

The door to my lab opened and shut. I pretended I didn't hear anything.

Whoever it was, couldn't they see I was working? Hopefully, they would have the common sense to leave me alone. Didn't they know how important my work was?

"Leena," came a soft voice. Melodic. Mariella.

I didn't want to talk to her.

Last time she came in, she tried to get me to leave. She wanted me to go to sleep.

Didn't she understand that I couldn't do that? Every moment I wasn't working, memories flooded my brain and suffocated me. Even seeing the Xathi simulation on my monitor made me feel like I had a mouthful of blood.

I avoided looking at the simulation itself. I focused on the results. The results were all that mattered.

Something good had to come out of all that horror.

"Leena!" Mariella said in a harsher voice.

I knew that voice. She rarely used it, but when she did, she meant business.

"I'm busy, Mari," I said dismissively.

I heard her footsteps. Assuming she was leaving, as any intelligent person would have, I paid her no mind.

Suddenly, all of my monitors went black. The overhead lab lights flickered on. They were so bright, I had to squint just to see anything.

"Mariella, what the fuck?" I screeched, whirling around.

I moved too quickly. Black dots populated my vision, and the world tipped a little bit.

Mariella reached and grabbed me by the shoulders.

Probably to keep me from falling over, but also to keep me from bolting. Mari was smarter than she let on.

"I've had enough of this," she snapped.

"Somebody's got to try to find a cure for our illness," I shot back.

"Don't even pretend that's what this is about," Mariella scoffed. "You're using your dead-end research as an excuse to run away from everything."

"So what if I am?"

I tried to wrench my arms out of her grip, but she was stronger.

When did my baby sister become stronger than me? I rarely stood this close to her. When I did, I was always taken aback by the fact that she was taller than me.

"And it's not dead-end," I added, sounding like a petulant child.

"You're right," she sighed. "I'm sorry I said that. I was frustrated. But Leena, listen to me. You're going to make yourself sick if you keep this up. Have you even eaten today?"

No, I hadn't, and I don't think I ate yesterday, either. It was hard to tell. All of the days blurred together in the lab.

"Turn my monitors back on, please," I said weakly.

"No," Mariella replied firmly. "Not until you hear everything that's happened."

"I don't need to hear about it," I seethed. "I was there."

"Not for all of it," Mariella argued. "Do you know what happened when you passed out?"

I tried to tune her out. I didn't want to think about it.

I remembered the blood.

There was so much blood on the floor, and Axtin was in the center of it.

No one could survive that kind of blood loss.

"I don't—"

"I know you think you don't want to know," Mariella said gently, completing my own thought, "but you need to. Tu'ver told me everything. When you passed out, Axtin picked you up and carried you. He fought the Xathi with you in his arms, shielding you from it all. He brought you outside. Thankfully, reinforcements had gotten there in time. And then he went back in. He continued charging through the Xathi ship until he was certain every human that survived was out. Even the doctors in the med bay don't know how he did it. The blood loss should have rendered him unconscious before he even made it out with you."

"How many are still alive?" I asked. I didn't recognize the grave, hollow voice that came out of me.

Mariella didn't answer right away.

"Mari, tell me how many," I said through gritted teeth.

"Sixty-nine," she replied softly. She looked at her feet.

"Sixty-nine," I croaked. From one hundred. I'd failed so many of them.

"They are all alive because of Axtin," Mariella said quickly. "He refused to stop until he knew he saved everyone he could have saved."

"He did what I couldn't," I murmured.

"Leena, stop that! Don't you dare blame yourself for what happened."

Mariella shook me gently. The world spun once more.

"You and Axtin, I swear. You're acting like children, thinking the world is on your shoulders."

Children.

Oh no.

"Where's Calixta?" I whispered.

"Who?" Mariella asked, her brow wrinkling in confusion.

Dread settled in my stomach. If Mariella didn't know who I was talking about that meant she…Calixta was…

"Oh! The little girl?" Mariella said brightly. "I didn't realize that was her name. She's here on the *Vengeance*.

She doesn't say much, poor thing, I think she's quite shaken up. And who could blame her after everything?"

"She's alive," I whispered and stumbled back into my chair.

With a wrenching pain, the icy wall I'd built around my heart crumbled. I was repulsed with myself for locking myself away in the lab so that I could pretend that my research and results were all that mattered in the world.

"She's a sweet little thing too," Mariella repeated. "She made paper flowers for Tu'ver, Axtin, and everyone else who helped get her out of that ship."

"That sounds like her," I said, a faint smile on my lips.

"Has she asked about me?"

"She checks your room in the med bay every day, even though she knows you won't be there. She doesn't know where else to look, and I think she's too shy to ask anyone." A familiar smirk twisted Mariella's lips. "Pity you're too busy to spend time with her."

"She knows a lot more than she lets on," I mused. "I have to go see her."

"Anything to get you out of this lab," she chuckled, following after me at a more leisurely pace.

"Wait," I paused suddenly. The words Mariella said earlier clicked in my brain like magnets snapping together. "Did you say something about Axtin?"

"Yes," Mariella nodded, a small smile tugging at the corner of her mouth. "I said you both are stubborn fools who've convinced yourselves the weight of the world rests on your shoulders."

"You spoke to him?" I asked, the words forming slowly.

I'd already forced myself to emotionally let him go. The way he looked so lifeless in the med bay, I made myself let go of all hope that he would wake up.

"Yes, not too long ago, actually," she said, eyes sparkling with amusement.

"You care about him, Leena. It's okay to admit it. Liking someone makes you vulnerable, that's true." She nodded as if she knew more than she was letting on but didn't elaborate. "But after everything, I think Axtin's earned your trust, hasn't he? Do you really think he would do anything else but protect you?"

Logically, Mariella made very solid points. Axtin had risked his life for me multiple times since the day we met.

For the most part, I'd been a prickly bitch towards him. Though I still suspected he liked pushing my buttons. And I had to admit, I liked my buttons being pushed every now and then.

But the feelings that stirred in my chest when I thought of him were so wonderful and warm that the thought of losing them paralyzed me with fear. I would rather never experience the full effect of those feelings than get comfortable and have it all taken away.

"Mari, I'm scared," I whispered as tears pricked at the backs of my eyes. "I don't want to see him. It's too much!"

Mariella closed the distance between us and wrapped me up in a hug.

"Of course, you're scared, Leena," she said running a hand along the back of my hair just like our mother used to do when Mariella woke up from a bad dream.

Just like I used to do for her after our mother died. Just like I did to comfort Calixta in the dark room on the Xathi ship.

"But you're not the only one who's scared. All of us are terrified out of our minds. And that's okay."

"You're scared?" I asked her.

I found it hard to believe. For so long she seemed so at peace with everything in her world, even in our illness.

"Yes," she admitted. "But I know that when I'm scared, there are people around me who will help me through it. People like you and Tu'ver. You've just got to learn to let people support you, that's all."

She gave off a small laugh.

"Oh, is that all?" I chuckled dryly.

I pulled back from our hug to wipe a tear off my cheek.

"Let's tackle that in baby steps, eh? I need to check on Calixta," I said.

Before Mariella could speak, the lab doors flew open.

"Leena!" A familiar voice that I never expected to hear again called out to me.

Axtin.

AXTIN

In hindsight, I realized that crashing into the lab of a recently traumatized woman probably wasn't the brightest idea, but I had been hard-pressed to think of another option at the time.

I stood in the doorway, my eyes pulling immediately to where Leena stood. Her eyes widened as she saw me.

I opened my mouth to speak, only to find myself at a loss for words. The last time I had seen her, I had been badly injured, crouched and bleeding at her feet.

I stuttered, trying desperately think of how to start. How could I possibly express to this woman how terrified I had been when I'd discovered she was captured? How could I even begin to verbalize that fury I felt at the thought of her being hurt?

I had no idea where to begin.

Mariella saved me the trouble.

"Axtin," she said, her eyes widening in surprise. "What are you doing? How'd you get out of your restraints?"

I glanced down at my wrists, noting the friction burns now winding around them. Turns out, once I finished waking up, the bonds weren't as strong as I'd initially thought.

There were a lot of things that needed to be said right now, and how I managed to get out of med bay wasn't one of them.

"I need to talk to you." I said, directing my gaze toward Leena.

Leena stared across at me, emotions I had no idea how to name washing over her face.

"Axtin," Mariella hissed, drawing my eyes to her. She walked over to me. "I told you to let me talk to her."

"I know, and I appreciate you trying, but there are things I need to say myself... things Leena needs to hear."

She hesitated, turning to look at Leena before putting her attention back on me. "I don't know, Axtin."

I suppressed my frustration. "Trust me."

"She's really fragile right now." She bit her lip nervously.

"I know, I can handle it."

"Really—" she tried one last time before I cut her off.

"I can handle it, Mariella," I declared with finality.

She stood still a moment longer, her forehead creased in thought.

Finally, just when I decided she wasn't going to budge, she nodded. "Okay." She sighed. "I hope you know what you're doing."

"I do."

She turned back to Leena. "I'll be down the hall if you need anything."

With that, she finally left. I waited silently until I heard the door shut behind her.

Leena had turned back to her computer, her back facing me as I approached. I moved slowly and carefully, as if I were approaching a frightened animal. In a way, I guess I was.

Mariella was right about one thing, Leena was fragile right now. The absolute last thing I wanted was to make things harder for her.

"Leena," I said, keeping my voice low, "are you okay?"

She didn't respond, didn't even move.

I walked closer, reaching a hand out to her. I didn't know how she'd react to being touched just then, but my body practically screamed at me to do it. I needed to feel her, to know that she was alright.

It was all I could do not to grab her and pull her into my arms.

"Leena." I tried again, letting my hand fall softly to her shoulder.

She spun the moment it did, surprising me as she whipped around to face me. I had expected her to be frightened, angry, but the woman that turned to me was neither of those things.

Her face was alight, eyes shining beautifully as they skimmed over my face.

"You're okay," she whispered.

I cupped her cheek, marveling again at the softness of her skin. How sweet she was behind her walls. How perfect. "Now that I've seen you, yes."

"Axtin!" Her voice cracked on the word.

She threw herself into my arms, her hands wrapping around my neck as she pulled me desperately into a kiss.

The moment my lips met hers, everything else faded away. I sunk into it, pulling her against me frantically.

Her hands roved over me, exploring me as if she was looking for holes. Given what we recently went through, she might have been.

She pulled back, meeting my eyes once again. Her eyes brimmed with tears even as her lips pulled into the most radiant smile.

"It's okay," I offered, running my hand along her cheek, down the curve of her neck. "We're all okay."

That was all it took. Her dam broke at my words,

her face collapsing into tears. She leaned into me, burying her face against my chest as she sobbed.

Hearing her cry broke my heart. I ran my fingers through her hair, offering small words of comfort here and there, but mostly just letting her collapse into me.

She had been through so much... so much pain that she didn't deserve. No one did, of course, but least of all my Leena.

I wished that I could have spared her from it, kept her safe from all the horror she'd had to witness—all the fear. I had wanted to, and I had failed. Her tears were a vivid reminder.

All I could do was be here, hold her and let her fall apart.

Her tears finally slowed and her shoulders relaxed. Still, I held her for a long while even after she had grown quiet.

It was her who eventually pulled back, frantically wiping at her eyes as she gazed up at me. I reached for her hand, stopping it mid swipe and pulling it back down to her side.

Then, slowly, I ran my thumbs under her eyes, catching the tears that she had missed. She smiled as I finished. It started small, timid, but grew the longer she looked at me.

"I was so worried." She ran her hand along my midsection.

I knew what she saw as she did, what awful images were replaying in her mind. I couldn't imagine how hard it must have been for her to see me like that, bleeding out right before her. If the roles had been reversed, I probably would have lost my mind.

"I'm healed now, Leena," I assured her.

She nodded, but the doubt in her eyes didn't fade.

"You don't have to worry anymore. I'm here for you. Do you understand?"

She reached up, taking my face into her hands. Her thumbs ran small circles over my cheeks, her eyes falling to my mouth.

"I know," she said.

And then her lips were on mine again. Her kiss was still frantic, still wild, but now focused in her intensity. The tension eased from her body, the fear ebbing as my tongue slipped between her lips.

I had wanted to be gentle, to wait, to take things easy. It only seemed right, after all. The moment that I actually had her again, though, gentle was the last thing on my mind.

My cock throbbed as I lifted her from the floor, pulling her against me in a desperate rush.

The feel of her in my arms was intoxicating. After all the fear, the close calls and near deaths, I had her again. I never wanted to let her go.

She kissed me eagerly, already pulling at my shirt as I carried her to the nearest desk.

I settled her onto it, pulling at her clothes even as she continued to tear at mine. It didn't take long before there was nothing left between us.

I lowered myself onto her, my hand running up her leg as my lips found her neck, her throat, her collarbone. I worked my way slowly down, tasting every inch of her, biting and sucking in equal measure.

My mouth wrapped around her nipple, pulling at her as my tongue circled. She let out a moan, her body quivering beneath me.

"Oh god, Axtin," she groaned, "I missed you so much! Don't ever do that to me again!"

I let her nipple fall from my lips, rising up until I was again facing her. I had never wanted anyone so much as I wanted her in that moment. She gazed up at me, her eyes seeming to burn from within.

"I swear on the systems Leena," I declared, "I will not."

I kissed her again, slower this time, with all the force of a promise. I realized, of course, that I couldn't guarantee that nothing would happen to me again. It wasn't exactly my lot in life to live safely.

I could however, do everything in my power to stick around. And I would.

I hadn't had anything worth living for in quite a

while. I'd had causes worth dying for. I'd had reasons to sacrifice.

But reasons to live? Those had been taken from me years ago. Now that I had another, I wasn't planning to leave this place anytime soon.

Leena pulled me close to her, the full press of her body driving me to madness.

It was insane that, just days ago, I had thought I might never be able to feel this again, might never get to be with her again.

Sometimes, life throws you good surprises.

As I spread her legs beneath me, watching her squirm with anticipation, I decided that she was by far the best.

Because Leena was nothing if not surprising.

LEENA

The nightmares continued in the days that followed, not always exactly the same as the one from med bay, but near enough. I woke up most nights in a cold sweat, images of the Xathi swarming through my mind as I fought to catch my breath.

The big difference was that I no longer woke alone.

I slept in Axtin's cabin every night, content that even if the dreams came, he'd be there to comfort me.

And it wasn't just a one-way street. I woke several times to him thrashing at my side, his body struggling to fight off whatever monsters his mind was conjuring. More often than not, they were the same monsters as my own, Xathi soldiers, sub-queens.

Even though we'd escaped from them, they still wouldn't let us be.

I'd wake him gently, holding him as he adjusted back to reality. Sometimes he'd come back to me quickly, other nights would take a while. He'd clear his eyes as he processed his surroundings and would smile at me then, as grateful for my presence as I was for his.

We settled into a routine, relaxing as best we could in the relative safety of the ship. I never felt entirely at peace, though, how could I, knowing that the Xathi were still out there? But I began to function again, to plan, and for me that was good enough.

During the day, while Axtin was off with General Rouhr and the others, I busied myself in the lab, trying my utmost to perfect the scent bombs.

I still wasn't satisfied with them. The ones we had concocted so far were effective, but I believed I could make them even better. I *knew* we could.

After days of trial and error, I had finally started to make progress.

I had found ways to subtly alter the chemical compounds from the original scent bombs. With my new formulas, we could make different kinds. Stronger ones for the more formidable of the Xathi, the sub-queens for example, bigger, wider-range bombs for large groups.

With the new variety of weapons, I thought we might stand a better chance the next time we went up against the Xathi.

The thought still made my heart race, my palms sweat, but I was working through it. I knew that sooner or later, the day would come for another fight. Likely sooner.

Since there was nothing I could do to stop it, I had resolved to be prepared.

After spending time amongst them, I finally understood the full scope of the threat we faced. I finally understood what Axtin and the others had been up against for so long.

They'd been the only ones left to fight the Xathi where they came from, all of them having watched as their planets fell prey to the monsters.

It was illuminating really, seeing them in action. I now knew what drove Axtin to be the man he was, what fueled the fire in him that burned so brightly.

He hadn't been able to save his planet, he hadn't stood a chance.

None of them had.

Now though, they had an opportunity to save others. To spare a new planet from the terror of the Xathi.

I intended to help them do it, pouring all of my energy into the cause.

Days after we had returned to the ship, I sat in the lab, as I did so often, my eyes skimming over the notes projected before me. I was finally content with my work on the scent bombs. The new iterations would give us an edge, something the Xathi wouldn't see coming.

I checked and rechecked the formulas, going over my own documents with a fine-tooth comb.

It all checked out, my new formulas were ready.

I added final notes to the files, saving them for later use. We would need to get started on production immediately, there were just a few new ingredients I needed.

I closed the final file, leaning back with a sigh.

That was it then, my contribution to the cause, all neat and bundled up. I only hoped that it would be enough to turn the tide in the war.

The true test wouldn't be done in a lab after all, but in the middle of battle, while people's lives hung in the balance.

I stared blankly at the screen; I tried to suppress memories flashing brightly through my mind.

It would have to be enough, that's all there was to it.

I moved to switch off the console when an unfamiliar file caught my eye. I hadn't noticed it before, being too focused on my research. But I saw something I hadn't added to the memory.

It must have been uploaded by mistake; it was from a completely separate branch of the university than my own research.

With a swipe of my hand I opened it, preparing to press delete when something caught my eye. A simple phrase really, but it stilled me nonetheless.

Beginning stages of immunodeficiency it read.

I leaned in closer, my eyes skimming over the list that now filled the screen. As I read on, more phrases jumped out at me, more symptoms.

They were achingly familiar.

Of course they were, I had thought about these particular ailments every day of my adult life.

My hand went to my mouth, my eyes widening in shock. There before me, plain in black and white, was a description of my condition, the genetic disease that even now lay dormant inside me.

My hand shook as I reached to swipe further down the page, the blood beginning to rush through my veins.

It was all there, every indicator, every painful symptom.

I read to the bottom, hoping beyond hope for some new tidbit of information. I found it in the last line, the first new piece of information I had come across in my years of research.

Likely cause: long-term exposure to toxic gas, N.O.X.

I let out a breath I hadn't realized I'd been holding, my whole body seeming to relax as I finished reading.

This was it, finally a lead.

I had never heard of N.O.X. before, not even a single mention of it in my studies, but as I stared unblinkingly at the letters, I felt a renewed sense of hope begin to build inside me.

If this were true, if our condition really was caused by exposure to a toxic gas, then we might be able to find a cure yet.

My head spun, a million thoughts blinking to life in my mind. I was so caught up, it took me a moment to come to the most important of them.

I had to tell Mariella.

I jumped from my chair, hearing it strike the wall with the force of my movement. I didn't bother to stop and right it, I was already running for the door.

I pulled it open, flying through the entry and into the hall.

After several minutes of searching, I finally found her, standing in a hall with Tu'ver.

"Mariella," I cried, rushing towards them, "Mariella, I've found something, you need to come with me!"

She turned, looking genuinely perplexed as her eyes fell on my smiling face.

"Leena, are you okay?"

I waved her concern away with the flick of my wrist, reaching down to take her hand.

"Yes, I'm fine. Better than, actually. I need to show you something. Right now."

She hesitated a moment, flashing Tu'ver a look of complete and utter confusion before finally relenting and following. I pulled her at a near run, dodging her questions as we made our way back to the lab.

I can only imagine how insane I must have looked, eyes wide, manic smile on my face, but I didn't care. It would be worth looking like a fool, the moment Mariella saw the file.

I dragged her into the lab, finally letting go of her hand in order to right the fallen chair. I pulled it back to the monitor, gesturing at it with my free hand.

"Sit."

"Leena, what is going on?"

"Just sit." I said. "Look."

She raised her eyebrows in question but did as I asked, glancing casually towards the screen.

"You've…made a list of our symptoms?" she asked, turning to look at me

"No, not me. Just keep reading."

She turned back to the screen, her shoulders slumping as she read over the dire symptom list that she already knew too well.

I saw the moment she got past it, the very second that her eyes found the final sentence. Her shoulders tensed, her hand pausing mid-air as she leaned in for a better look.

"Gas?" she finally said, her voice an octave higher than usual.

"Yes, something called N.O.X. Have you ever heard of it?"

She shook her head, eyes still glued to the screen.

"No, I haven't. Leena, do you think this could be true?"

"I do. Mariella, this could be our answer!"

She sat another moment in stunned silence, her eyes tracing over the sentence again and again. When she had apparently assured herself it was real, she stopped, turning in her chair to face me.

She wore a grin to match my own, her eyes burning with anticipation. "It's there. In the files. You found it." She sprung up, arms wrapping around me with impressive force, squeezing the air from my lungs.

I didn't mind, I hugged her back with equal vigor.

After a long moment, she pulled back, wiping at the tears that now brimmed her eyes. "I didn't think there was any hope."

"I know, it's okay, Mariella."

"No, it's not okay. I gave up, on a cure, on us. I should've known you'd find something eventually."

I stopped her mid-rant, silencing her with an upraised hand. "Nothing's for sure yet, Mariella, it's only a chance."

She nodded, taking my hand. "I know, but it's more

than I thought we had. We'll figure this out together. I mean, hell, I'm an archivist. Finding information is kind of my job."

I smiled up at her, squeezing her hand as tears stung at my own eyes.

"Okay, then," I gestured towards the chair, "let's get started."

AXTIN

I had never felt such peace as I did in the days after waking up in med bay. I had never felt such calm.

I knew that it was Leena's doing.

What else could it have been? Nothing else in my life had changed, not really.

From the moment I woke up, life around the *Vengeance* had been much the same. The halls still seemed to bustle with activity, the crew still vibrated with anxious energy, plans were being made, threats assessed. From all appearances, it was life as normal, but something about me seemed to have changed.

I was calmer, more thoughtful. My mind still wandered often to the Xathi, but that was no longer the only place it traveled. I found myself thinking of things that I hadn't in years, pleasant things—things that revolved chiefly around Leena.

I still woke occasionally to nightmares, long-buried memories that forced themselves out in the dead of sleep. It was nothing new, not for anyone aboard the *Vengeance*.

The days that we could rely on peaceful sleep were long gone, burned up with our families and our planets. I suppose that stood true, but for me, they had started to come less often.

For me, Leena was now there to pull me out of them, to remind me that things had changed since those days.

This was a new life.

A new planet.

And even though we weren't yet free of the Xathi, we were no longer playing at such a great disadvantage.

We were making sure of that, more so with every passing day.

Leena spent her afternoons holed up in the lab, working tirelessly on new and improved scent bombs to use against the Xathi. I, for my part, was also working relentlessly.

There was always something new to learn about the enemy, always another plan to go through. My days were spent in command, working with General Rouhr and the others, desperately trying for any advantage.

We were approaching the problem from all sides now, no longer only relying on passion and determination to see us through. Sure, we had all wanted the Xathi dead before coming here, but that hadn't been enough, not really.

We had been desperate men, the last of our respective species.

Nothing left to fight for but our revenge, nothing to protect but ourselves. It was no way to live.

It was no way to fight.

Desperate men might've had nothing left to lose, but they'd also had nothing real to hope for. That had all changed in the days since our arrival. We were approaching things from a new perspective now, one of strength rather than desperation.

For the first time in a long time, I felt that we might really have a chance.

We had to be different now, better. There was another planet at risk, countless more lives.

After years of doing, we were stalled, thinking before acting.

To be completely honest, there were moments where it was all but infuriating, but they were fewer than we might have expected. In a way, it was freeing to act like more than soldiers for once. Most days, anyway.

It didn't help that my physical training had hit a

roadblock. Recovering from my injuries had been slow and painful. I still trained to the best of my ability, but it was a weak imitation of my prior self. I couldn't yet swing my hammer, could hardly keep up with Vrehx on runs.

Still, the doctors assured me I would heal with time, that there shouldn't be any lasting damage. Most of the time I believed them, sometimes my impatience got the better of me. I was eager to be back to my full strength, to feel capable again.

On the bad days, Leena was there. She reassured me, she encouraged me, and perhaps most importantly, she distracted me.

When training became too much, I would head over to the lab to spend some time with her.

At first, it was enough just to watch her work. She was amazing, the depth of her understanding blew me away. Sometimes I'd ask questions, trying my best to follow along with her explanations.

Most days I'd just watch in utter fascination as she built weapons from next to nothing.

After a while, I became even more interested in the process, offering my help whenever I saw an opportunity. Leena, of course, was only too happy to put me to work.

She was amazing at the science of it all, the chemistry. But I soon found that I had a lot to offer to the task. I might not have understood it all, but building came to me like a second nature.

For hours at a time, we would sit together, me assembling the bombs while Leena worked at her concoctions. She had already come up with several new versions of the originals, each seeming more effective than the last.

With her help, I felt like real progress was being made.

As much as I loved my physical training, I started to really look forward to those days together. I had spent so much of my life as a weapon; it was like I had forgotten I could be anything else.

It was typical of my species, the Valorni were almost always dismissed as brutes. With our stature and natural talent for warfare, I suppose it wasn't exactly an unfair assumption, but we could be so much more than soldiers.

It was just one more thing that Leena reminded me of.

On a day not long after I had begun to assemble the bombs, Leena and I sat in the lab, talking over a pile of equipment. By this point, she had started to trust in my abilities, no longer watching me like a hawk as I pieced together the weapons.

She had been busy triple-checking a formula when

she suddenly sighed, sinking into her chair with a look on her face like defeat.

"What is it," I asked. "What's wrong?"

She leaned forward, propping her elbows on the desk and resting her head in her hands.

"Will it be enough?" she finally asked, not bothering to turn to me.

"The bombs?"

She sat up, "Yes, the bombs. All of it. Do you think it will be enough?"

I wanted to say yes, to reassure her immediately. But I knew Leena well enough to know that anything other than the truth would be pointless. She could smell a lie from a mile away, especially on me.

I stood from my chair, crossing the room to kneel in front of her. "I don't know."

She nodded as if she'd been expecting the answer.

"Some days it feels like it won't."

I knew what she meant. Some days it all felt almost pointless to me, as well. Those were the bad days, the ones where everything seemed so bleak.

"I have those days, too."

"Often?"

I thought on it, running my hand through my hair as I did so. "Less often than I used to." I answered, reaching for her hand.

A small smile tugged at her lips, "And before?"

That was easy enough to remember, "Before, I don't think I ever believed anything could be enough, not really. Back then, the most I hoped for was to take out as many Xathi beasts as I could before they dragged me down with them."

She didn't pretend to be surprised at that, having witnessed it first hand when we first landed. She just tightened her grip on my hand, leaning down to press a kiss to my lips.

"I'm glad you don't feel that way anymore."

So was I.

"I really do think that we can beat them, Leena. Just look what we're accomplishing here," I gestured around the room. "This matters. This could make all the difference."

She sat silently for a long moment, the wheels in her mind clearly turning. Finally, she nodded again, sitting up straighter in her chair and looking around the lab.

"Well then, I guess we better get back to work."

EPILOGUE: LEENA

The sound of leaves crunching underfoot was almost a comfort after so many days spent in the lab. I'd half forgotten how nice the sun felt, how clean the air was.

For a while after the attack, I thought I might never be able to leave the safety of the ship again, or Axtin, for that matter. But as the days drew on, my strength started to come back. After a while, I was practically itching to get out.

I wasn't alone. Vidia and the other survivors were also struggling to adjust to life on board the *Vengeance*, used to far different accommodations as they were.

After a while, they had started to plan trips outside. Nowhere far, of course, but out in the fresh air. Vidia had arranged most of them, still leading in

her own unique way. She'd worked a compromise
with General Rouhr to create an outer enclosure,
safe from the native terrors, still shielded from the
Xathi.

At first, I'd reluctantly gone with Axtin, feeling
responsible for Vidia and the few survivors after all that
we had been through together. After that, it just became
another part of the routine.

I turned to Tu'ver, smiling as he scanned the forests
for threats. He, like all the rest of the crew, had become
very protective of the new human contingent.

"I think we're okay," I said, drawing his attention to
me, "I can still see the ship."

He scoffed. "I'm not about to get lazy because of it.
It's not worth the risk."

"I don't think there are any Xathi nearby," I chided.

"It's Axtin I'm worried about. If I let something
happen to you, he'd kill me for sure."

I laughed loudly, startling birds from the trees. After
a while he joined in, though we both knew he was
probably right.

It had been like pulling teeth just to get Axtin to let
me go outside without him. He'd been busy with
General Rouhr and insisted I wait until tomorrow. Of
course, he finally relented, but only on the condition
that I take Tu'ver along.

I'd pretended to be bothered, but really, I was

grateful. I might have been ready to go outside again, but being alone still frightened me.

Tu'ver didn't make me feel quite as safe as Axtin, nobody did, but he was a close second. I knew beyond a shadow of a doubt that he would gladly put himself in harm's way for us. He was just a good man like that—or alien, rather.

I felt a tug at my hand and turned, smiling down at Calixta. She, too, was growing used to the crew of the *Vengeance*. She still occasionally shied away from Tu'ver and Vrehx, but Axtin had already grown on her.

In the first days that Calixta started living with us, she was still a bit leery of him, which was only natural, after watching him obliterate a Xathi with his hammer, but he had worn her down over time.

Now she had his big green heart wrapped around her tiny fingers, and he couldn't be happier.

"Are we almost there?" she asked, looking around impatiently.

Our outings with the refugees were one of her favorite pastimes. The *Vengeance* might have been her new home, but she still looked forward to the days she could spend outside with the other children.

"Actually," I said, pushing my way between some densely packed trees, "we're here now!"

She laughed as she ran into the clearing, greeting the refugees by name.

"Stay where I can see you!" I reminded her, jogging to keep up.

I saw Vidia a moment after Calixta did, and she ran to the woman, throwing her arms around her in greeting.

"Leena, Calixta!" Vidia called. "There you are."

From my side, Tu'ver cleared his throat.

"And Tu'ver," she added, "always a pleasure."

"Likewise."

I crossed to the older woman, giving her a hug before turning to look at the refugees.

"How is everyone doing?" I asked, nodding to a group of children. Calixta had already inserted herself amongst them, laughing along to a joke none of us could hear.

"They're doing well. Some people are still struggling, but we're making do as well as we can."

Her voice hinted there might be more to the story.

"Vidia... how are things really going?"

She sighed, looking down at her feet. "Things are as well as could be expected," she finally offered, "given the circumstances."

"What's been happening?"

"Oh nothing," she said with a wave of her hand. "I do worry some about the psychological effects of what they've all been through. I'd be a fool not to. But everyone's trying, we're all working to get past it."

I nodded, unsure of what to say. Long-term psychological effects would hardly be surprising, given what we'd all been through.

"And you?" I finally asked

She smiled, "I'm quite well, Leena."

"You know, if there's ever—"

She interrupted with a grin. "Anything I need, I can ask you. Yes, I know. We all do, dear. It's just going to take some time to adjust."

I opened my mouth to question her further but she stilled me with a raised hand.

"Enough shop talk," she said, "I promise, our problems will all still be here tomorrow. Right now, that girl of yours seems to require your attention."

I turned to find Calixta waving her arms. "Leena, Tu'ver, come play with us."

HOURS LATER, we walked back into the *Vengeance*, Calixta now asleep on my hip.

I said goodbye to Tu'ver, and tucked Calixta into bed before heading off to find Axtin.

He looked up as I walked into the training area, a smile pulling at his lips.

"How was the clearing?"

"Exhausting." I said, crossing to him.

He laughed, reaching out to pluck a leaf from my hair, "I'll bet."

I looked him up and down, noting his heavy breathing as he set his weapon aside.

"Have you been training since we left?"

He had the decency to look abashed.

"Maybe."

"Axtin," I scolded, "you know you can't push yourself too hard."

"I'm not, I swear. I was just about to stop."

I raised a brow in disbelief. "I'm sure."

He chuckled, "Well, I'm stopping now."

"I see that, but you still can't—"

"Oh please," he chided, "if I didn't bring you food most days you'd probably starve to death in your lab."

I opened my mouth to argue but only a laugh came out. He had a point. It was easy for me to forget things like food and water when I was working.

"Touché."

"Have you eaten today?" he asked, his expression suggesting he already knew the answer.

"Maybe I'm hungry for other things." I ran my hands up the broad planes of his chest then back down, curling my fingers until my nails lightly scratched him.

"You tempt me, mate," he growled, tugging me to him.

I blinked, pushed against him to lean back while my mind reeled.

Mate?

I stared at him.

Not when facing the Xathi, not when rescuing the prisoners, had I ever seen such a look of fear on Axtin's face.

We hadn't exactly made plans for the future, just settled into our routine.

But...

I leaned forward and nibbled at his lower lip until he relaxed into me.

"And I plan to keep tempting you." I locked his gaze with mine. "Mate."

LETTER FROM ELIN

I don't have favorite couples, I really don't!

But if I did, Axtin and Leena would be near the top. They're so much fun together, each so stubborn in their own ways - and magic when they learn to work together.

Next up?

If you know you're going to die young, you can react in a few ways.

Harden your heart. Fight destiny.

Or roll with the hand you're dealt and enjoy what time you have.

Archivist Mariella thought all hope of a cure for her disease had been lost long before the Xathi invaded.

The war sped up her timeline, nothing more.

The warriors of the Vengeance? Friends only.

Even if one of them calls to her heart and sparks new desires within her...

Tu'ver and the rest of the K'ver esteem logic and order above all.

He has a function.

To fight with the crew of the Vengeance. To kill the Xathi. To avenge his people.

So why is he so drawn to the gentle human, Mariella?

And when there's a chance to obtain information that may save her life, why would he risk everything to save her?

In the war between Logic and Passion, there can be only one victor.

Get Tu'ver now!

https://elinwynbooks.com/conquered-world-alien-romance/

XOXO,

Elin

T u'ver

"AARGH!"

Sylor had stealthily waited in a corner, unnoticed as Axtin passed him by in the mess hall. The resulting sound he had made startled Axtin to the point of nearly dropping his tray.

I hid a smile and watched as Axtin 'threatened' Sylor and Sylor returned the threat with a compliment about Leena.

It was surprisingly entertaining.

We found ourselves eating together more often, the two teams that had infiltrated the Xathi ship to rescue Leena and the other humans. Sylor was interesting to listen to when he relaxed. A match for Axtin in the bravado department, almost a match for me in games of skill, and a match for some of the humans in terms of demented humor. And Karzin was a Valorni version of Vrehx, just much louder.

Two weeks had passed since the rescue, and tensions were high. The Xathi had been on edge since our infiltration of their ship, and it had forced us to be on edge ourselves.

Axtin turned his attention back to the table. "Duvest only has so much room for the refugees. We're about maxed out here as well. With the Xathi raiding everything that moves including the plants, what are we supposed to do?"

Vrehx shook his head. This had been the topic at hand for the last eight days, ever since Thribb told the Captain that our ship's system couldn't handle this many people for much longer. With nearly a hundred extra digestive systems using the facilities, our recycling systems, compromised as they were due to our crash on this strange world, were taxed to the limit.

With a heavy breath, Vrehx looked at Axtin, opened his mouth...and shut it again with a shrug. "I don't know. We've been able to keep pathways to Duvest and Einhiv open, and Sk'lar's team has found a set of tunnels that lead to Fraga...but since Fraga's been destroyed, the tunnels are essentially useless." He looked at his plate, moving his food around with his knife, then, apparently tired with eating, pushed his plate away and stood up. "I don't know, Axtin. I just don't know."

It was Daxion that spoke up, stopping Axtin from saying something undoubtedly brash. "We'll find a way, we always do."

Vrehx gave him a thankful nod and paced around the mess hall. The idea that we had brought the Xathi to this world and caused them to be targeted by one of the worst threats in the galaxy weighed on him heavily, as it did all of us.

Daxion and Sakev bid us a good evening and left. It was their turn for patrol and they wanted to get a few hours of sleep before they went out. That left Axtin, myself, and the pacing Vrehx to sit in the mess hall.

Axtin looked at me and asked. "And?"

Slightly confused, I nodded at him and arched my eyebrow.

"You've been quiet, which isn't anything new with you, but even you join in the conversation when it involves work. So…what's on your mind?"

I opened my mouth to answer but was interrupted by Vrehx sitting down. He motioned for me to continue and I did. "I've simply been trying to work some things out. I've been thinking about our current situation with the refugees, the Xathi, and our munitions."

"Oh? What about our munitions?" Axtin asked. Trust him to pick up on anything involving his weapons.

"We've blown through about ten percent of our supply in the months since we crashed. That means we'll be out of ammo within a year based on the way the Xathi have been acting lately."

"Koso!" Axtin swore.

"I've been thinking about how to conserve them, but it would involve more of us in close combat. I'll be honest with you, I'm not particularly fond of the idea of getting close to the Xathi. Not all of us have the tough skin of the Valorni or a Skotan's scales," I said as I pointed at Vrehx.

He nodded and lightly flexed his scales into view, then smiled. "So, if things come down to it, we'll figure out which ones are better for hand-to-whatever combat and which ones are better at shooting, then we'll adjust."

Axtin smiled, flexed his muscles, and winked at me. "Don't worry Tu'ver, I'll protect you from the big, bad bugs. I'll just smash them all to pieces with my hammer."

At my chuckle, the other two laughed.

"Didn't realize you were developing a sense of humor," Axtin cracked.

The assassin inside of me, who had suppressed his

emotions for so long and expected others to do the same took umbrage.

But I had observed my crewmates, these other species, for a long time now. There was apparently something therapeutic about sharing humor.

We spent the next thirty or so minutes talking about everything and nothing, mostly nothing.

Oddly, it felt good to be included, to be part of the group. I had been the last one to join the crew, and although we had been around one another for almost a year, it had always been a professional relationship based strictly on stopping the Xathi.

I wasn't the only one thinking of the changes. "Do you two think we would have done this if we hadn't come here?" Axtin grabbed the last of the food from my plate.

"Done what?" Vrehx sipped his drink.

"*This.* This whole conversation where we sit here in the midst of a war, talk, do more than just tolerate one another."

Vrehx and I looked at one another, both of us apparently sharing the same look on our face because Axtin failed miserably at stifling a laugh. Another round of laughter ended with Axtin wiping tears from his eyes and Vrehx trying to catch his breath.

It felt...nice to let go.

Before I could stop myself, I took a deep breath, then struggled for the right words.

"What is it?" Vrehx asked.

Void. I wasn't a child. I barged straight ahead. "I'm not quite sure how to broach this subject, but I was wondering about your relationships with the human women."

"What about them?" Axtin raised his eyebrows.

"How is it that you've found a way to make them work? What I mean is, how do you look past the difference in species?"

Both looked at me, visibly trying to hide their grins. I regretted opening my mouth. I should never have asked these two fools this question.

It was Axtin that broke the silence first. "You like Mariella." It was a statement, and the lilt of his voice suggested that he was amused by the idea. "I knew there was something a little *special* about the way you looked at her, especially when you carried her."

"You did seem to take to her right away. You even ignored my orders," Vrehx added.

I looked at him in shock. "I'm sorry, Commander, but I do not remember you giving me an order."

"You were a little preoccupied." He turned to Axtin with a knowing look on his face. "You know? I think he was the first one to fall for one of the women."

"I think you're right. Our little Tu'ver was the first to fall in love. Aww."

They broke out into another round of laughter while I sat there. Could they be right? Did I 'fall' for Mariella right away?

Vrehx stopped laughing and put his hand on my shoulder. "I'm sorry, we don't mean to make you feel bad." I must have looked particularly dour, but he continued. "To answer your original question, once I got used to Jeneva's...personality...the fact that she's human didn't matter to me."

Axtin chimed in with a grin. "Yeah, her *personality* sure won you over. She's got a nice *personality* when she walks past." He laughed and ducked as Vrehx threw a gentle Skotan punch.

Maybe not so gentle.

"At least he's being complimentary," I said.

Vrehx turned back to me. "Jeneva's been good for me. I still want to defeat the Xathi, but now it's because I want to save her, us, and whoever else is out there from the Xathi. I want revenge, don't get me wrong, but that's not what drives me anymore, and that makes me feel good. She makes me feel good."

"Vrehx has a point." Axtin leaned forward, his smile still there, but voice serious. "Jeneva has been good for him, and Leena has been unbelievable for me. I wish to be worthy of her. I know that she's temperamental. I never really know if she's going to kiss me, kick me, or kill me, but that's what adds to our relationship. She'd be a fantastic Valorni."

"That she would," Vrehx agreed.

They were right. The women *had* changed them, and for the better.

Axtin's training was more controlled, less chaotic. Even his actions during patrol were more calculated, as if he wanted to make sure he did his job to the best of his ability.

Vrehx was calmer, less stringent about the rules and more willing to adapt to his team instead of trying to make us adapt to him.

What had Mariella done to me?

I'd always been calculated, 'slow' according to the old Axtin. I'd always been deliberate in my actions. None of that had changed, nor could I imagine it would.

So, what had Mariella done to me except make me feel a sense of separation when we were apart and a sense of joy when we were together?

Not sure about my own feelings, I thanked the two of them and excused myself.

Perhaps it was time to bury the assassin that Tu'ver had been.

And find a way to enter into a partnership with Mariella.

MARIELLA

"Do human men look strange to you now?"

I turned my head at the sound of Jeneva's voice, even though the question wasn't directed at me. She sat on top of a black storage crate, her back pressed against the wall and her head resting lazily on her shoulder to look at my sister.

Leena thought for a moment before a wicked grin spread across her face.

"Human men have always looked strange to me," she quipped. I giggled from my spot on the floor, my back pressed against the end of the same crate that Jeneva sat on. Jeneva threw her head back and laughed a full belly laugh, her chin length hair bouncing around her face. Leena sat at a small table we had scrounged up a few weeks back.

Looking between the two of them, I couldn't believe how much they'd changed, Leena especially. If someone told me a year ago, hell even a month ago, that Leena would be laughing and joking with friends, I wouldn't believe them. I would have sooner believed that an alien spaceship would fall through the sky bringing with it, species both fascinating and terrible.

As the universe would have it, both happened.

I didn't know Jeneva very well, but she was so different from the bristly, reclusive person I'd met in the forest when everything first changed. That person, though she did save my life, wanted nothing to do with anyone. Now, Jeneva sought out company whenever she could. She laughed often and loudly and never ran out of things to say.

It was her sister, Amira, who was now the bristly, reclusive one. Part of the reason why we were hanging in a spot in the refugee section of the *Vengeance* was so Jeneva could spend time with Amira. The ship that felt more like home every day, but Amira refused to leave the refugee wing whenever she could help it.

I didn't know the whole story between the two of them, but now that I'd reconciled with Leena, I deeply regretted the time we spent apart, especially after we lost our mother. I would tell Amira as much, she was still a bit prickly. She'd figure it out on her own.

Another woman, Vidia, occasionally joined our little group. The former mayor of a town that had been destroyed by the Xathi. she had become the de facto leader of the refugees. I had never been to the town, but I heard it had been beautiful. Vidia and roughly a hundred others were the only survivors of that bustling town.

One of those survivors was a little girl, Calixta, Leena's little shadow now. A little bit less so now that'd she'd found a friend to play with, but we all loved having her around.

"What do you think about human men, Mariella?" Jeneva asked me, drawing me back to the here and now.

"All the boys used to love Mariella," Leena answered for me with a knowing smile. "But my sweet sister never gave them the time of day. She was always happier in the library anyway."

I blushed and looked at my hands. It was true, I often turned down dates growing up and in school. The truth was, I never found any of them even remotely interesting. I couldn't be more specific if I tried. They were all just missing...*something*.

"Now she only has eyes for Tu'ver," Leena teased. I could hear a note of unease in her voice, though she was trying to hide it.

I ignored it, tucking a strand of hair behind my ear.

"She's not even trying to deny it," Jeneva chimed in, her tone much warmer than my sisters.

"He's my friend," I said unconvincingly. It was the truth. He was a K'ver and not much of a talker, but I preferred his company to almost anyone else. Though I'd been barely conscious at the time, I still remembered how he carried me out of the dank cave deep in the forest after a spider-like aramirion nearly gutted me.

Tu'ver visited me in the med bay almost every day after that. He was the one who had fitted me with the transmitting device I still wore in my ear, though it was no longer necessary for us to understand each other.

If I was ever able to get back to my own work, the device would be invaluable. Because of it, I could now speak Tu'ver's language, albeit clumsily. He could speak mine as well. When we spoke, we drifted between one language and the other almost without realizing.

I was comfortable with him in a way I didn't feel with anyone else, not even Leena.

Leena scowled, then had the decency to look embarrassed. "Sorry, Mari. There's just something about him that makes me worry about you spending too much time with him."

"He's not the friendliest," Jeneva agreed.

"He saved all of our lives," I argued.

"That's true and we're grateful for that," Leena placated me. "But even Axtin knows to give Tu'ver a wide berth - and that's saying something."

"I think it's sweet that you like him," Jeneva smiled. "He sure seems to like you. You're the only one he tolerates for an extended period."

I didn't want to admit to either of them how much that idea appealed to me.

"Can we talk about something else?" I asked, twirling a lock of my dark waves between my fingers.

"Leena said something about you spending time in libraries. Is that what you were before all of this happened? A librarian?" Jeneva asked, looking around the refugee bay.

"An archivist," I corrected with a smile. It was a common mistake many made. I never took it personally. Jeneva's brow furrowed in confusion, another common reaction.

I launched into my well-rehearsed explanation. "Most of my work is translating. There were many languages on old Earth. Some of our most important works are in another language entirely. I also track down original paper documents that have yet to be converted to digital."

"I can't remember the last time I saw something written on paper," Jeneva mused.

"Many of the original field surveys from the time of settlement were completed during a period when the electronic systems were still unstable," I answered. "Not all of the details were transcribed into digital later."

There were a few museums in the larger cities. They were the only places members of the public could view relics like paper documents. I had access to most of the private collections on this world. My favorite was an old library containing nearly a hundred full paper books. I'd been working on transcribing one of them to digital form when my sister showed up at my door.

If she hadn't dragged me into the middle of the jungle that day, we would have never met Jeneva. We probably would have died that day.

"How did you fall into that?" Jeneva asked, tilting

her head. I admired her natural curiosity, especially after she spent so long repressing it.

"Originally it was to complement Leena's work," I replied. In the corner of my eye, I saw Leena go a stiff in the shoulders. I was coming too close to talking about our shared secret.

The illness that killed our mother.

Personally, I didn't mind talking about it. I didn't go out of my way to tell people but if someone asked me a direct question I wouldn't lie.

Leena hated the idea of anyone knowing about it. She didn't want to be pitied. Besides me, the only person on the ship who knew about the illness was Axtin, the Valorni male that adored my sister.

"How so?" Jeneva pressed, oblivious to Leena's growing unease.

"Leena and I share many interests, if you can believe it," I answered, choosing my words carefully. "Our research was similar, though our fields were different. She covered the biological and chemical aspect. I searched for answers through our history. We figured we increased our chances of uncovering something remarkable if we worked together." There was a gleam of excitement in Jeneva's eyes.

"Were you close? What were you looking for?" She asked.

"Mariella," Leena said through clenched teeth.

Jeneva looked to Leena, then back to me.

"Leena, I think we should just tell her," I said with a sigh. "She's a friend. What do you think is going to happen if she knows?" Leena chewed on her bottom lip as she thought it over. Eventually, she sighed, dropping her shoulders and giving me a nod of approval.

"Leena and I have a rare genetic illness," I said, turning my attention back to Jeneva.

Her jaw dropped, and her eyes filled with genuine sadness for us. "That must be awful," she said. "Is it..." She let her voice trail off, but I knew what she meant to ask.

"Yes, it's fatal," I explained. "Leena and I have spent most of our adult lives trying to cure it. More so Leena, that me," I admitted. There was a time where I wanted nothing to do with finding a cure. It was too hard to hope for something that might never happen.

"I'm so sorry," Jeneva said, her voice barely more than a whisper. This was the pity Leena hated. She didn't like to feel weak. I didn't like seeing Jeneva like this because I didn't like the idea of needlessly causing another person to worry. It wasn't Jeneva's fault that I had this illness and it wasn't on her to cure it. She shouldn't have to worry on our behalf. Leena and I worried plenty.

"But we've made a breakthrough recently," Leena cut in. "There's something on this world called N.O.X.

I'm not sure what it is exactly, but I accidentally found someone's medical record who came in contact with N.O.X. They showcased many of the same symptoms as the later stages of our illness."

"That's amazing!" Jeneva's face lit up. "So, you think you can cure it?"

"If the universe wants it," I said with a smile and shrug. It was a motto, of sorts. Losing my mother and discovering the illness that lived within me made me feel scared and out of control for a long time.

I had to teach myself that the only way to move past that fear was to give up control. It was easier than I thought it would be. Once I considered how vast the universe was and how small I was in comparison, I found it easier to simply *be*.

When I was still in school, I came across the works of an author who lived on Earth long before my time, long before planetary colonization was even close to possible. His name was Arthur C. Clarke and, centuries ago, he spoke the words that I carry with me now, always.

Magic is just science we don't understand yet.

I believe in that magic.

"I should go," Leena said, bringing me out of my thoughts. "I told Axtin I would have dinner with him tonight, but I have to get some work done at the lab if I'm going to make that happen." She gave me a squeeze on the shoulder before leaving the refugee bay.

"I should get back to work as well," Jeneva said apologetically. She'd been keeping busy recording information about useful properties of the local plants.

I felt useless. Everyone else had an important job to do on the *Vengeance*. I was mostly left to my own devices.

At least all that free time enabled me to make plenty of friends. I knew most of the refugees by name. Same with the *Vengeance* crew.

I preferred talking with the various species found in the crew. Their worlds were fascinating. I could scarcely wrap my head around the fact that they came from a corner of the galaxy that we had no idea existed until the rift tore through everything that separated us.

I got to my feet as Jeneva left, planning on seeking out Tu'ver. It was late enough in the day that he'd probably be done with his shift. Hopefully, he was in the mood for some company. Though even if he wasn't, he wouldn't tell me.

"Wait." A thin hand grabbed my arm as I made my way toward the exit. I stopped, though the hand that grabbed me didn't have the force behind it to stop even a child. The woman who grabbed removed her hand, clutching it to her chest.

Her face was familiar, as all the human faces were

now, but I had never spoken to her. She was quiet and kept to herself for the most part. She was thinner than she should be. There was plenty of food to go around now that the food replicators were powered back up.

"Is everything okay?" I asked gently when she didn't say anything more.

"You and your sister," she said, her voice halting and stuttering. "You say you're sick?"

"Yes," I answered honestly. "But it's a genetic illness. It's not contagious," I explained quickly. I could understand why the thought of an illness breaking out in the refugee bay would cause alarm.

"I know," the woman said.

I blinked in surprise. "I've always been a good listener."

"What do you mean?" I asked.

"I'm old and frail," the woman continued without shame. "Most people usually ignore me or don't even notice. So, I listen to the conversations of others to keep me company."

I nodded. She must have overheard everything.

"I heard you two with your friend," she said to me, confirming my own thoughts. "You're sick and you don't know why."

I nodded my head slowly.

"It's not contagious," I repeated, trying to allay her fears.

"And no one knows anything of your illness," she continued, ignoring me.

She was right.

After all this time, Leena and I had never managed to find a documented case of the illness. The woman stared at me, her eyes slightly glassy. I could tell she had been through horrific things before she found her way to the *Vengeance*.

"But," she continued, now looking at me intently. "I might know something about it."

TU'VER

As the doors to my quarters opened, I realized how happy I was that my shift was over. When we aren't out in the world, my job on the ship is to maintain the ship's defensive systems.

I enjoyed my work...manipulating electronics to create more proficient ways to kill came easily to me.

But my conversation with Axtin and Vrehx put me in a sour mood, and having to constantly find parts, or wires, or circuits, or micro-chips to make sure the defensive systems stayed working without proper manufacturing facilities was becoming monotonous and annoying.

As much as I enjoyed my solitude, the task was occasionally wearing.

My room was simple, a bunk on the far wall, a desk near the door, and a makeshift kitchen that I made for myself out of spare parts, wood from the trees we knocked down when we crashed, and a pair of heating coils from some broken Scrappers. We used the hovercrafts planetside, and I constantly needed to repair them.

I looked in my cooling unit, pondering what I was in the mood for. I pulled out some meat, some vegetables, and the spices I needed and began to cook.

Yes, there was a mess hall and food replicators, but cooking in my quarters had always been a task that allowed me a chance to focus my thoughts.

This had been true for my entire life. On the *Vengeance*, I had set up an informal system with the galley master. I upgraded his equipment from time to time and he passed me over a small amount of the meat that he used for meals that would have been used for my portion anyway.

Meat took a substantial amount of energy to replicate so it seemed like a fair exchange for my services. I also procured certain vegetables from the hydroponics lab and lately, Jeneva had introduced me to local vegetables that wouldn't try to eat me - as certain plants on this planet did - as well.

I remembered back to my first two years in the service. They were terrible. I was reassigned six times, each time in a different corner of the world, and each time with a commanding officer that was fundamentally different than the one before. At times, cooking my own meals had helped me get through the drudgery.

Being moved from assignment to assignment didn't lend itself to creating lasting friendships. I was always reserved around others, more so than even most other K'veri. Most of my time when not carrying out my duties was spent in solitude. I preferred it that way.

Those around me knew to give me a wide berth. There were always rumors about the extent of the training that the military had subjected me to.

If they only knew.

If anything, their conceptions only scratched the surface.

My training had been exhaustive. It had been brutal. And it had been effective.

Even on the *Vengeance*, I knew that regardless of what I was doing, I stood a greater chance to kill another living being than almost anyone on this ship. I didn't have the outward swagger of Axtin or the sense of danger that Vrehx embodied, but my cool, rational nature allowed me to pinpoint an enemy's weakness and exploit it in the shortest amount of time.

I had seen so much killing even in my live training

exercises that solitude became preferable to anything else.

Until now.

Now...it almost seemed that Mariella was able to reach through the self-imposed exile I had sent myself into and speak directly to me.

Humans were fragile compared to K'veri. Mariella was more so. But that only seemed to whet the appetite that she brought out in me.

I had served aboard this ship through multiple engagements. I had seen countless battles.

But now I had encountered an enemy towards my solitude that my training had not prepared me for.

My mind was in a tumult. Years of routine created through rational self-exploration were now being turned on their head.

I needed to resolve this. Soon.

I finished cooking my meat and mixed in my vegetables. If it hadn't been for Jeneva, I never would have tried carrot and never would have known that the mickelania root was as tasty as it was. It looked horrible, like something from a creature's bowels, but it tasted fantastic. It was a bit tart, but if cooked in Tilemmin broth, the tartness was tempered and became mouthwatering.

My sister had taught me how to use Tilemmin broth to cook our vegetables. Thinking of her brought a sad smile to face, and I promptly burned my finger. The sudden pain snapped me back to reality.

I bandaged myself and looked at my meal. Without realizing it, I had made Cannira's favorite meal. She always ate Tilemmin stew when she had big news.

She was a lot like Mariella, maybe that was why I liked Mariella so much.

But Cannira was no longer alive. I had failed to save her.

And that's when I realized why I had been silent around Mariella for so long. Why my attraction had been something to suppress rather than inflame.

I feared that in the moment, I would be unable to save Mariella too if she were to get too close.

Perhaps it was time to change that type of thinking and take a gamble.

GET TU'VER NOW!

https://elinwynbooks.com/conquered-world-alien-romance/

PLEASE DON'T FORGET TO LEAVE A REVIEW!

Readers rely on your opinions, and your review can help others decide on what books they read. Make sure your opinion is heard and leave a review where you purchased this book! http://getbook.at/Axtin

Don't miss a new release! You can sign up for release alerts at both Amazon and Bookbub:
    bookbub.com/authors/elin-wyn
    amazon.com/author/elinwyn

For a free short story, opportunities for advance review copies, release news and the occasional cat picture, please join the newsletter!
    https://elinwynbooks.com/newsletter-signup/

And don't forget the Facebook group, where I post sneak peeks of chapters and covers!

https://www.facebook.com/groups/ElinWyn/

DON'T MISS THE STAR BREED!

Given: Star Breed Book One

When a renegade thief and a genetically enhanced mercenary collide, space gets a whole lot hotter!

Thief Kara Shimsi has learned three lessons well - keep her head down, her fingers light, and her tithes to the syndicate paid on time.

But now a failed heist has earned her a death sentence - a one-way ticket to the toxic Waste outside the dome. Her only chance is a deal with the syndicate's most ruthless enforcer, a wolfish mountain of genetically-modified muscle named Davien.

The thought makes her body tingle with dread-or is it heat?

Mercenary Davien has one focus: do whatever is necessary to get the credits to get off this backwater mining colony and back into space. The last thing he wants is a smart-mouthed thief - even if she does have the clue he needs to hunt down whoever attacked the floating lab he and his created brothers called home.

Caring is a liability. Desire is a commodity. And love could get you killed.

https://elinwynbooks.com/star-breed/

ABOUT THE AUTHOR

I love old movies – *To Catch a Thief, Notorious, All About Eve* — and anything with Katherine Hepburn in it. Clever, elegant people doing clever, elegant things.

I'm a hopeless romantic.

And I love science fiction and the promise of space.

So it makes perfect sense to me to try to merge all of those loves into a new science fiction world, where dashing heroes and lovely ladies have adventures, get into trouble, and find their true love in the stars!

Printed by Amazon Italia Logistica S.r.l.
Torrazza Piemonte (TO), Italy

16747593R00181